Leading Lady

Also by Jane Aiken Hodge

Fiction

MAULEVER HALL
THE ADVENTURES
WATCH THE WALL, MY DARLING
HERE COMES A CANDLE
THE WINDING STAIR
GREEK WEDDING
MARRY IN HASTE
SAVANNAH PURCHASE
STRANGERS IN COMPANY
SHADOW OF A LADY
ONE WAY TO VENICE
REBEL HEIRESS
RUNAWAY BRIDE
JUDAS FLOWERING
RED SKY AT NIGHT
LAST ACT
WIDE IS THE WATER
THE LOST GARDEN
SECRET ISLAND
POLONAISE
FIRST NIGHT

Non-Fiction

THE DOUBLE LIFE OF JANE AUSTEN
THE PRIVATE WORLD OF GEORGETTE HEYER

JANE AIKEN HODGE

Leading Lady

G. P. PUTNAM'S SONS
NEW YORK

G. P. Putnam's Sons
Publishers Since 1838
200 Madison Avenue
New York, NY 10016

Library of Congress Cataloging-in-Publication Data

Hodge, Jane Aiken.
Leading lady / Jane Aiken Hodge. — 1st American ed.
p.   cm.
I. Title.
PS3558.O342L4   1990   90-8215 CIP
813'.54—dc20
ISBN 0-399-13562-6

Printed in the United States of America
1   2   3   4   5   6   7   8   9   10

This book is printed on acid-free paper.

Leading Lady

1

Princess Martha was playing truant. Instead of ordering a carriage for the ten-minute drive down the winding mountain road from Lissenberg's palace to its opera house, she had slipped quietly out by a side-door of the palace to take the steep footpath across the vineyards. It was good to be out, better still to be alone, away from the unspoken questions that hummed through the palace corridors.

The grapes were dark on the vines now, almost ready for harvest; they had been small green clusters when she and her husband had last come this way, the day before he left for France. But she had come out to forget her troubles. She shrugged them away and reached out to pick a ripe grape from a bunch temptingly close to the path.

'Hey!' The angry voice startled but did not alarm her. She turned, smiling, to face the man who had come out from between the vine rows just behind her. He was dressed in the smock and fustian breeches of a fieldworker but his stance and tone suggested a foreman or overseer as he shouted angrily at her in Liss. American herself, she was learning the language of her new country fast, but was still often baffled by the broader versions of the local accent.

But everyone in Lissenberg spoke German. 'I'm sorry,' she smiled her friendly smile. 'But I am your landlord, you know, just sampling the crop.'

'Landlord?' A sharp look, not a friendly one. Then: 'The devil, so you are! Hey, boys!' He raised his voice. 'Look who's here!' They grew their vines high in Lissenberg and Martha, who had thought the vineyard deserted, now saw her mistake as sun-bronzed workers emerged here and there from among the vines to which they had been giving a late pruning. Some held knives, others small sickles that gleamed in the sun. She fought cold terror as they closed around her on the narrow path. Most

7

of them were naked to the waist, glowing with sweat in the hot sun; she smelled them as they came closer.

'The Princess herself,' the overseer went on. 'Just the person we want to talk to. Right, boys?' A low growl of assent. They were too close now; she backed up against a small wayside shrine by the path. 'About our wages, see, highness.' A note of mockery in the title? 'When that husband of yours comes back, that surprise, Prince Franz. If he does come back! You tell him we want the same pay as the miners at Brundt he sets such store by. Raised their pay when they asked for it this spring, didn't he? And you doling out comforts for the women, and not a Lissmark for us.'

'I'm sorry. I didn't know.'

'Why should you? No affair of yours. A woman! But I'm telling you now, since Prince Franz saw fit to leave you in charge here.' His tone was sceptical, and a voice chimed in from the crowd: 'Prince Gustav wouldn't have, that's for sure.' Other voices joined in, disturbingly unintelligible, in Liss. They were working themselves up. To what?

She must not show she was afraid. She held herself very straight, caught and held the overseer's eye. 'That's enough,' she said. 'Get your men back to work and I'll look into your grievances.'

There was a short little horrid silence while she found herself glad for the first time that she was not beautiful. If crowd frenzy won, and they attacked, they would have to kill her. To die, here in the hot sun . . . Unbelievable . . . Never see Franz . . . The long moment extended, the muttering grew, they were pressing closer, then, from the back of the crowd, a new voice: 'Hey! Here come the women with our lunch!'

The threatening crowd broke up, dissolving among the vines, and Martha turned without another word and walked back up the hill to the palace. Re-entering by the door from which she had emerged with such a cheerful sense of holiday, she was glad to get to her own rooms without meeting anyone. Her maid and ally, Anna, had had leave to spend the night with her mother down in the little town of Lissenberg, and it had been partly with the idea of meeting her on her way back that Martha had started out on what had proved such a dangerous venture. Anna would think nothing of walking

8

up through the vineyards. But Anna was a Lissenberger born and bred. Martha was shaking now as she thought of the danger she had escaped. It had been touch and go, and she knew it.

She knew too that she would tell no one about it, not even Anna. It was sad to think that she would never walk alone again. Not in Lissenberg, the country that had acclaimed her as its princess only a year ago. What had gone wrong? And would she tell Franz when he got back? But then, when would Franz get back? And why had there been no messenger? She was back in the vicious circle of worry she had tried to escape when she set out on her unlucky walk. She would do something about the men's wages, of course, but she had learned a grim lesson.

She had herself well in hand by the time Anna returned. 'What news in town?' Casually.

'Nothing special. My mother sends her respectful greetings.' They had first met when Martha had discovered the wretched conditions in which Anna's mother worked, long before she became Princess of Lissenberg. 'But what about up here?' Anna went on eagerly. 'Has a messenger come from Lake Constance?' Lissenberg's only road to the outside world ran past the palace and over a mountain pass to Lake Constance.

'Nothing. You'd think we were cut off from the world as we are in winter. He must have written, Anna.'

'Of course he has, highness! Something's happened to the messenger, that's all. You know what the roads are like all over Europe after all the years of war there. I sometimes wonder if we Lissenbergers are grateful enough for living at peace as we do. Mother says they are grumbling in Brundt again. It's hot even in the mines, this weather . . .'

'It must be, poor things. But – grumbling, Anna?' With their pay just raised, she thought.

'I wish Prince Franz would come home.'

'Not half as much as I do.' Her laugh was dangerously close to tears. 'I miss him so!'

'Of course you do. And with Lady Cristabel also away. When do they get back, highness, the opera company? They're being sadly missed in town.'

'I know.' It had been to enquire about this that she had

started on her unlucky walk. 'We all miss them sadly.' Bread and circuses, she thought. Did she dare raise the labourers' wages while Franz was away? Did she dare not? What was happening in Lissenberg? She moved restlessly to the window to look for the messenger who did not come. 'I wish the palace wasn't so far out of town. It's not good to be out of touch like this.'

'I suppose Prince Gustav thought it safer.'

'For a tyrant, yes. But you know my Franz wants to rule as a democratic prince.' Her voice warmed as she spoke of her husband who had found himself turned, all in one night, from revolutionary leader to reigning prince. Then, suddenly: 'Look, Anna! Dust on the horizon; there's a carriage coming. If only it's Franz!'

'I do hope it is.' Anna had been more worried by the state of things in Lissenberg than she had admitted to her friend and mistress. 'No, it's the opera company!' Her eyes saw better than Martha's which were still blurred with tears.

'Oh, well, that's something, I suppose.' Martha made an effort at cheerfulness. 'Send a message to the hostel, Anna. Ask Lady Cristabel to come to me just as soon as she can. I long to hear how the tour has gone, and she is bound to have news of the outside world.'

'And of Prince Maximilian in Vienna. I do wonder . . . I'll send at once, highness.'

Lady Cristabel arrived even sooner than Martha had hoped, as eager as her friend for the meeting. One long embrace and they drew back a little to look at each other.

'You look wonderful,' Martha said. 'The hot weather always did suit you. And the tour has been a tremendous success, from what I've heard. You've been sadly lacked here, I can tell you. Oh, Belle, I am so glad to see you. I've missed you so much.' Her friend was more beautiful than ever, she thought, dark ringlets glossy, amazing blue eyes shining, and a glow of happiness over all. She would not spoil it, yet, with her own anxieties.

'I've missed you too.' Cristabel did not feel she could return Martha's compliment. 'You've lost weight! It's elegant, but is it such hard work being Princess of Lissenberg?'

10

'It's not easy. But then, nothing that's worth while ever is. And you know what a struggle my poor Franz had last winter, trying to make the Lissenbergers accept him as the democratic prince he wants to be. Strange to get rid of a tyrant like Prince Gustav, and then expect tyranny from the democrat who replaced him.' She could not forget the workmen's reference to Prince Gustav, deposed prince and attempted murderer.

'They're a strange lot the Lissenbergers. Poor Franz! Fancy mounting a democratic rebellion and then finding himself the legitimate prince all the time. It must have been a sad come down for him. But how is he? Worked to death as usual? I long to tell him of the success we have had with his opera. The world is mad for *Crusader Prince*.'

'He's away, I'm afraid. I'm surprised you've not heard. He will be sad not to have been here to welcome you, hear all about the tour.' Before he had become, so surprisingly, Prince of Lissenberg, her husband had been a successful composer of operas, as well as a revolutionary. 'But, tell me, Belle, did you see Max, when you were in Vienna? And his opera, *Daughter of Odin*? Is it going to be as brilliant as they say?'

Cristabel made a little face. 'There is talk of a wild success – that Germanic stuff is all the rage just now. Frankly, not just our kind of music. As to Prince Maximilian, yes indeed we saw him. He's well. Treading the tightrope between court and musical society with his usual grace. I've a letter from him for Franz, and all kinds of messages. Remarkable how well those twin brothers manage to get on after finding each other so late.'

'Yes,' Martha agreed. 'I think it does them both the greatest credit, but specially Max, who had always thought himself the heir to Lissenberg.'

'He still says he'd much rather write opera. I think he means it, but it's hard to tell with Max.'

'I hope *Daughter of Odin* really is a success!' Martha was increasingly aware of a tension in Cristabel, under the glowing exterior, surely greater than the occasion warranted. She was glad that she had seen to it that they met first in private. 'Cristabel, you keep saying "we"?'

'Yes.' Cristabel, the prima donna who could hold an

11

audience in the palm of her hand, was blushing now like a schoolgirl. 'Martha, do, please, be happy for me. I'm married, Martha, like you.'

'Married?' For a moment she let herself hope that the old romance with her husband's twin, Prince Maximilian, had revived in Vienna. 'Cristabel, who is it?'

'Who could it be but Desmond?' Cristabel's tone belied the confident words.

'Desmond Fylde?' Martha could not keep the shock out of her voice. 'Your Irish tenor?' What could she say? She had neither liked nor trusted Desmond Fylde when he had played opposite Cristabel in the triumphant performance of *Crusader Prince* that had ended in revolution in Lissenberg, and her husband on its throne. The man who had then been plain Franz Wengel had written the opera as part of his planned revolt against Lissenberg's tyrant, Prince Gustav, only to discover that he himself was twin heir to the principality. Acknowledged by his brother, Prince Maximilian, and acclaimed by the crowds, he had insisted on an open election and won it with ease.

That September of 1804, nearly a year ago, it had all been romance and roses. Franz had married Martha, his American heiress, on a wave of popular enthusiasm, and his brother, Prince Max, had gone off to Vienna, to work on his own opera, *Daughter of Odin*, at the Burgtheater. Martha had always hoped that one day Max and Cristabel would find their way back into the childhood romance that had been shattered by Napoleon's intervention. Now she could only look at her friend with a kind of mute horror.

'My Irish *prince*.' Cristabel emphasised the last word. 'Do, please, rejoice with me, Martha.' The note of pleading went to Martha's heart. Could she, already, be having doubts about the 'Irish prince' whom Martha's knowledgeable friend Ishmael Brodski had described as an adventurer from the Dublin slums?

'What does Lady Helen say?' Martha went straight to the point. She herself had been Cristabel's backer and adviser during the years of her training as a singer, before Lissenberg and *Crusader Prince* had made her a star. She had been (she faced it now) a little anxious when her friend went off on tour

12

with the too handsome tenor playing opposite her, but had counted on Cristabel's fierce Aunt Helen, sister of the Duke of Sarum, to keep him in line.

'You haven't heard?' Surprised. 'My father invited her home to England for the christening.'

'And she went?' Anger mixed with Martha's amazement. Lady Helen had been a voluntary partner in her bold and successful plan to make Cristabel into a prima donna. Her presence in the little party had been its guarantee of respectability. 'How could she?'

'How could she not? The heir to Sarum, after all these years.'

'I hope the divorce from your mother was through in time.' Martha could not help a note of wry amusement. She and Cristabel had discovered the mother everyone had thought dead, very much alive, in scandalous luxury at Venice. 'Have you written to your mother about your marriage?'

'No . . . not yet. It all happened so suddenly. Just the other day. Oh, Martha, it was the most romantic thing!'

'Tell me about it.' More and more, unhappily, she was aware of an insecurity in Cristabel. 'More romantic than my marriage?' She had been summoned up on to the stage of Lissenberg's opera house by its enthusiastic citizens to plight her troth, in public, to the man she had just learned was its prince.

'It was the day after Aunt Helen left.' Cristabel plunged into her story. 'The news came when we were at Salzburg. Such a romantic place – and a delightful audience! They had been starved of opera under the prince bishops. They went wild over *Crusader Prince*. Well, it's been a *succès de scandale* everywhere, of course. It's not every opera that starts a revolution.'

'And it's a good opera,' said Martha, whose husband had written it.

'Of course it is! Will he ever have time to write another, I wonder, your Prince Franz?'

It was something Martha wondered too. 'So – Lady Helen heard from the Duke,' she prompted.

'Yes. Pleased as punch; announcing an heir at last and asking her to stand godmother, along with Queen Charlotte. Well, Martha, you can see . . .'

13

'I can indeed.' Martha liked and respected Lady Helen, but, being American, had always been aware that she did not understand the English aristocracy. How odd, now, to find herself trying to pass as a princess. 'So, she left you? Just like that?'

'What else could she do? My father's letter had been delayed. There was no time to lose. The only thing was to hurry back to Vienna, decide there whether to take the northern route, or go south and home by sea. It's going to be a terrible journey either way, I'm afraid, with France and so much of Italy closed to the British.'

'And Bonaparte up at Boulogne, inspecting his invasion fleet,' said Martha.

'You must call him the Emperor Napoleon now.'

'Must I? And King of Italy? I wonder what your mother and Count Tafur think about that.' She came to one of her sudden decisions. 'Of course! I will invite them to come and pay us a visit, before winter cuts us off, here in Lissenberg. And I'll give them your news at the same time, shall I, Belle? But, first, tell me all about this romantic event.'

'It was after we left Salzburg, on our way to Munich. It was so strange without Aunt Helen. And you, Martha! It was always the three of us before. I hadn't thought I'd miss her so. Mr Fylde – Desmond very kindly offered to keep me company in my carriage.' She was blushing again, the vivid colour enhancing her brilliant looks. 'He said we had never had a chance to talk. It was true, you know, Aunt Helen was always there. Oh, Martha, when we were alone he said such things . . . How he worshipped me, adored me . . . His sun rises and sets in me . . . And then – we hadn't noticed, but our carriage had fallen behind the others – suddenly there was a crash, the coach rolled over. He saved me from harm, Martha, at the risk of his own life. We'd lost a wheel, crossing a tributary of the Salzach . . . No one in sight . . . We had to spend the night in a little hovel of an inn. He was so good to me, Martha, treated me like a princess. Not a word, not a look out of line.'

'And in the morning?' Martha kept her tone rigorously neutral.

'Such an unlucky chance . . . Well, not really, since the outcome is so happy. The carriage had been repaired overnight,

14

but it could not come up to the inn, the lane was too narrow, so we walked down, Desmond and I, and found it waiting, ready for us. But with another carriage beside it. Would you believe it? They were friends of Desmond's, singers in another troupe, bound the other way, for Vienna. They had recognised the carriage and stopped to see if they could be of any help. And there we were, the two of us, coming down from our inn, for all the world like Darby and Joan. The road was rough, Desmond had my arm, and I am sure I looked absolutely nohow when I saw them, standing there by the carriage. Desmond didn't lose his head for a minute. He pressed my arm, no time to say anything, greeted them with enthusiasm. And introduced me as his wife. No explanations, nothing, just the announcement. And then, of course, it was all kissing and congratulating, and I had a little time to recover myself. It was over in a few moments, none of us had any time to lose. Then, we were back in the carriage, Desmond holding my hand, apologising, asking me to forgive him. But what else could he have done? It was only anticipating a little, he said. When the accident happened he had been about to beg me to marry him in Munich, quietly, to avoid all the fuss and botheration it would mean if we waited until we got back here. He had a friend there, a Protestant minister, who would tie the knot. Now, he thought we had no alternative.'

'And you agreed?'

'Of course I agreed! I love him, Martha. And when we got there, his friend was kindness itself, arranged everything for us. Oh, it wasn't the wedding I'd meant to have – I suppose we all have our dreams. We just slipped off between rehearsals. Desmond said we wouldn't announce it till we got here, until I had told you and Franz. Then, you see, there can easily be a bit of confusion about whether it actually happened in Munich or back in Salzburg.'

'But you have been living as man and wife?' Martha went to the heart of the matter.

'Martha, we didn't mean to . . . I hadn't thought . . . Desmond behaved so perfectly all the way to Munich. Treated me like a queen. I think I'd assumed we'd wait . . . But then, by some strange chance, our rooms at the Munich inn were next door to each other, in a remote wing. It was hard to find.

When we got back late from the opera house, Desmond came with me, to show me the way. He opened the door for me, followed me in, kissed my hands, said I was his wife . . .' Her hands were twisting together in her lap. 'Then he kissed me. Our first kiss . . . And then . . .'

'I can imagine,' said Martha. 'And afterwards – at Ludwigsburg – what happened there?'

'Desmond said he could not bear to be parted from me. He arranged for adjacent rooms. He can manage anything, my Desmond. You will love him for my sake, won't you, Martha?'

'I'll do my very best.' What could Martha do but kiss her and promise? But in her heart, she put a very different gloss on the story. Altogether too many coincidences, too many obliging friends. Desmond Fylde had pushed Cristabel into marriage, but he had done it successfully. They had been living together, in the full public eye, for almost a month. 'Belle – ' How to ask it?

'Yes?' Something heart-rending about Cristabel's look of a child who expects to be scolded.

'You aren't by any chance increasing?' She got it out.

'Oh, no.' Cristabel was glad to be able to reassure her on this point. 'Desmond said . . . He thinks of everything, my Desmond. He says my career must come first for a while. He truly loves me, Martha, thinks of me. Says he wants to see the world at my feet.' She smiled, turned the tables on Martha. 'But you, Martha dear, have you any news for me?'

'No, alas. I'm afraid I am a sad disappointment to the Lissenbergers. Almost a year married, and still no sign of the heir they long for.'

'Well,' said Cristabel. 'If Franz stayed at home a little more. Or if you went with him on these foreign tours of his . . .'

'But how can he? And, come to that, how can I? You know how things are, here in Lissenberg. We have to face it that there are many in Franz's revolutionary party who were sadly disappointed to find that instead of an elected president they had got themselves a prince after all. I think, in many ways, he was disappointed himself but, once he found himself the heir, there was nothing for it but to make the best of things. No use pretending it's been easy this last year. Of course

16

he has had to visit the neighbouring courts, try for their approval, their support. And equally of course I have had to stay at home and run things here. He trusts me to do that. It's a great compliment.' She was beginning to wonder if it was one she deserved.

'One you have earned! But where is he this time? Surely he has reached agreement with the neighbours? They speak well of him in Bavaria and Württemberg, and Princess Amelia must have taken his part when she got home to Baden. I know she died in the end, poor lady, but you did save her life, you and Franz – and Max – when her husband was poisoning her. Tell me, Martha, how is the wicked Prince Gustav? Has Franz thought better of letting him retire to Gustavsberg? I always thought that an act of mad generosity. He's too dangerous a man to be let loose, that one.'

'I'm afraid I rather agree with you,' said Martha. 'But there has been no persuading Franz of it. He says Gustav's teeth are drawn; why spend money we cannot afford keeping him in prison, when banishing him to Gustavsberg will do just as well? I think an eye is kept on his visitors, and his mail, though Franz hates even that. He's such an idealist, dear man.'

'Crazy,' said Cristabel. 'In a world like ours. Where is he this time, Martha?'

'He's gone to France, to try and find out how Napoleon's mind is working.'

'Into the lion's mouth! The Emperor can hardly be best pleased with little Lissenberg since the way Prince Gustav turned against him after the murder of the Duc d'Enghien last year. But I remember Franz was a great admirer of Bonaparte's back in Paris when we were all there. Strange to think that he was a penniless young musician then and now he has gone back there as Prince of Lissenberg. How will you feel, Martha, if he returns to announce an alliance with France against England?'

'I must make myself feel as a Princess of Lissenberg should,' Martha told her. 'And I do beg you to help me, whatever your own feelings.'

'You can rely on me. I'm no politician as you well know. Desmond says the world of art has no frontiers, and I agree with him. And, as for you, Martha, after all, you're not British at all, but American; your country is an ancient ally of France.'

'I keep reminding myself of that, but just the same, I can't like what Napoleon is doing. Still less trust him. I shall feel much safer when Franz gets home.'

'At least he can't try and marry him to one of Josephine's nieces,' said Cristabel, whose own romance with Franz's brother had been abruptly broken off when Napoleon demanded that Max engage himself to Minette de Beauharnais, his wife's niece by her first marriage.

'No,' Martha smiled a little wryly. 'I do serve that useful purpose.' And then, quickly changing the subject: 'But aside from the great fact of your marriage, you've told me nothing about the tour, Belle, or Signor Franzosi's plans for the winter season.'

'Grandiose, as usual. Oh, Martha, I am disappointed Franz isn't here. I hadn't realised how much I had counted on him to make Franzosi see reason a bit, and, besides,' colouring, 'I thought he'd make the announcement about my marriage. He'd know just how to do it.'

'You'll have to make do with me.' Martha, too, had been wishing her husband was at home, to advise whether they should announce the marriage or insist it be annulled. But how could they do that? Desmond and Cristabel had been living together as man and wife for a month in the close conditions of a touring company. Desmond Fylde had played his cards too well. She thought there was nothing for it but to yield him the game, but with the darkest forebodings for the future. 'I shall give a celebration dinner tomorrow,' she said now. 'To mark your return. And make the announcement then. I doubt it will come as much of a surprise to the company.'

'No,' Cristabel admitted. 'There have been some knowing looks, I've thought. My Desmond adores me so, he says, it's hard for him not to let it show. He's singing better than ever, Martha.' She had seemed increasingly restless, now rose and moved over to the palace window. 'Oh, there's the carriage. He said he would come and fetch me. Martha, you will receive him, congratulate him?'

'Why – ' A tiny pause – 'Yes, of course.' Desmond Fylde's

next move had come even sooner than she had expected, but what else could she do but receive him?

He looked handsomer than ever, very sleek, very pleased with himself, and she disliked him even more than she had remembered. She kept the interview as short and as formal as possible. There were advantages, she was beginning to learn, about being a princess.

2

'Desmond, it's late!' Cristabel turned in the huge bed her husband had had installed in the star's apartments, for a quick glance at the clock. 'We must get up! The rehearsal begins in half an hour.'

'Ah, let them wait.' He reached out a casual arm to circle her waist and pull her down to him. 'You're the prima donna, my queen, let them practise their trills and tremolos without you; we have better things to do, you and I. We are owed a honeymoon, my angel. Franzosi should have more sense than to call us for rehearsal so early.' His other hand was busy at the neck of her nightgown. 'Why do you insist on wearing this high-buttoned garment in bed? To torment me?' He ripped a buttonhole, swore an oath she had not heard before. 'There!' A note of triumph as his questing fingers found her breast and caught it in a grip that both hurt and roused her.

'But, Desmond – ' She thought he had accepted that love in the morning left her unable to put her heart into her work. The high-necked nightgown had been meant as a tacit reminder of this.

'But, Bella – ' His tone at once imitated and faintly mocked hers. 'Must I remind you of a wife's first duty? To her husband, my own, to the husband who adores her; can't work, can't live, can't even think without her. My love!' He had got rid of the nightgown now and was kissing her leisurely here and there. As she felt herself gradually give way to his mastery, she felt also a small protesting voice somewhere deep down in her. What was it saying?

It was not the first time they had been late for rehearsal, but she had not previously been aware of the company's irritation, as well as Franzosi's. They were working on an opera he had written ready to celebrate Prince Franz's return, and she knew and regretted that she was doing less than justice to

20

her difficult part. It was not total comfort that her husband was superb in his.

If Martha had been tempted to tell Cristabel about that moment of terror among the vines, her marriage put it out of the question. She had raised the labourers' pay and got little thanks for it. The days dragged on, with still no word from Franz, and she felt more and more alone in her palace full of servants. She had hoped that her husband would return in time for the anniversary, on September 7th, of the night that had made him Prince of Lissenberg, but it came and went without any word either from him or from Cristabel's mother in Venice. Franz would most certainly return before winter closed the mountain road to Lake Constance. In her heart, she was sure he would be back before that, in time for their wedding anniversary in October, but she grew less and less hopeful of a visit from Cristabel's delightful, pleasure-loving mother and her long time lover, Count Tafur. Idiotic, really, to have hoped for it, when Lucia Aldini hardly troubled to stir from her luxurious Venetian palazzo except to visit the theatre and the opera house. Besides, what could anyone do for Cristabel, now that the marriage had been on public display for so long? Desmond Fylde had made it impossible for her to see Cristabel alone, but she was growing increasingly anxious about her. Anna had friends and cousins working both in the opera house and at the artists' hostel next door to it, and brought her the gossip from there.

'He makes her late for rehearsals.' Anna was tidying the bedroom. 'They don't like it, and of course she feels that and sings worse than ever.'

'Worse? Anna, what do you mean?'

'You haven't heard? No, I suppose you wouldn't have. It's just as well for her that the prince has been delayed. She's finding Franzosi's music difficult, they say, not singing her best at all. Some of them think he should have given her some time off, even if he wasn't consulted about the wedding, but naturally that made him angry. Herr Fylde is singing like an angel, they say. Well, he's got what he wanted. It would be a pity if this opera were triumph for him and disaster for her.'

21

'Surely he's got more sense than that?' Though she was a duke's daughter, Cristabel had no money of her own, her only prospects were in the opera house. Martha thought Desmond Fylde would remember this, fortune-hunter that she was sure he was.

'You'd think so. But some of us wonder if he really knows what he wants, that one. He's so certain he can charm the birds off the trees. Forgive me, highness, I'm talking too much.' She picked up an armful of petticoats and whisked herself out of the room before Martha could ask what she meant.

Martha was not sure she wanted to know. She was sitting, very rarely for her, doing nothing but brood about how to help Cristabel, when the sight of a carriage coming up the hill to the castle set her heart racing. Franz at last? No. As it drew nearer she swallowed sharp disappointment. Franz had driven off, most reluctantly, in his father's state coach; this was merely a gentleman's luxurious travelling carriage.

But whoever it was must be welcomed, and she was already busy making the necessary adjustments from lady at home to princess regnant when Anna reappeared to announce the Lord Chamberlain. Prince Franz had seen no reason to replace the majority of his father's court servants, and Baron Hals was gradually adjusting himself to the shocking informality of the new court. If he and Martha both remembered a night when he had condemned her to the ice-cold dungeons under the castle, neither of them referred to it.

'Highness,' he said now. 'An Italian gentleman is below, asking for you. A Count Tafur . . .'

'Alone?' But she should have expected this. 'I'll see him in the small withdrawing room, baron. He's an old friend of mine and Lady Cristabel's. You will see that he is comfortably lodged, of course. And,' an idea struck her. 'Send a message to Signor Franzosi at the opera house. Tell him I have an unexpected guest I'd like to entertain. A small, intimate performance tomorrow night? Something he has ready . . . Tell him I know I can count on him.'

'I congratulate you!' After the first greeting, Count Tafur looked her up and down with the friendly, quizzical glance she remembered so well. 'Every inch the princess. We were so sorry, Lucia and I, not to have been able to come to your wedding last autumn, but you know how she is. And this time, too, she thought it best to send me alone. Quite aside from her basic idleness, which we all know and love, she said you would find us an awkward enough couple to entertain. One of these days, perhaps, I shall persuade her to marry me, but I have not managed it yet. We are very well as we are, she says, and who am I to contradict her?'

'If only Cristabel had felt the same.' Martha was amazed to hear herself say it.

'It's as bad as that?'

'I'm afraid so. I'm more grateful than I can say to you for coming, though goodness knows what anyone can do for her . . . My friend and adviser Ishmael Brodski has made enquiries about Mr Fylde. There is a good deal that is shady about him, but no trace of a previous marriage to invalidate this one. He trapped her into it, count. I don't think there is the slightest doubt about that.' She plunged into the story, glad of the chance to tell it to this wise old friend who was as good as Cristabel's stepfather. And a great deal better than her father, she thought, as she told of the duke's invitation that had effectively removed Cristabel's one protection, the dragon aunt who had watched over her for so long.

'Lady Helen simply abandoned her niece at Salzburg?' Tafur was shocked too.

'It was irresistible, don't you see? To stand godmother alongside Queen Charlotte!'

'And Fylde saw his chance, and took it. You have to give him credit for quick planning. The poor child suspected nothing?'

'Not at the time, I think. She's always thrown herself so much into her singing; she's an innocent still in some ways. Lady Helen was the one who pointed that out to me.'

'Which makes her own behaviour now all the more inexcusable. But that's water under the bridge. The question is, what can we do now? If Cristabel were only a Catholic, I would hope for help from my friend the Pope, but as it is . . . Married by a Protestant minister at Munich, presumably with the blessing of the British representative there . . . Besides, would she agree?'

'Not yet! But it's affecting her singing, I'm told. I've asked for an opera tomorrow night, to celebrate your coming. You must judge for yourself.'

'And we must do nothing to throw her even more firmly into his arms,' said Tafur shrewdly. 'Does she know you sent for me – for us?'

'I called it a visit to celebrate her marriage.'

'Clever of you. Lucia sends you all kinds of love, by the way, and thanks for more care of her daughter than she has ever given.'

'Oh – ' Martha was surprised by a prickle of tears behind her eyes.

'And you?' Another of his shrewd looks. 'Do you enjoy being a princess? Do the Lissenbergers love you as they should? What a surprise that was! I do look forward to meeting your husband, lucky man. In every sense! Kingdom and bride at one swoop. I hope you expect him soon.'

'I wish I knew! I've not heard for a long while.' She was glad to share her anxiety. 'He's in France,' she explained. 'I can't help feeling anxious . . .'

'On more counts than one! But I really do not think you need be fearing anything like a repetition of Napoleon's murder of the Duc d'Enghien. He learned a lesson there, I am sure, though he will never admit it. He knows now that he must play the aristocrats' game more or less their way. And by all I've heard of him your Franz won't like that much either.'

'No. I worry about what Franz will do just as much. He made such a hero of Napoleon as the democratic leader he thought him. And now! Emperor of France, King of Italy, a court as full of pomp and ceremony as any in Europe . . . I made Franz promise to be careful what he said, but he does still come out with things. And I love him for it!'

'Not easy to find oneself a prince overnight,' said Tafur. 'And he did always sound a very positive young man, from what you and Cristabel said of him.'

Martha laughed. 'I thought him an intolerable bully when he was working on Cristabel's singing with her. What a long time ago it seems! Oh, it's good to see you. You'll stay a while, now you are here?' She asked it eagerly, and he was glad to see her looking more cheerful, more like the forthright young

American girl he and Lucia had grown to love quite as much as Lucia's own daughter. She had never been beautiful, but there had been a glow of intelligence about her that had been in some ways better than beauty. He had missed it when he first saw her, but it was back now, and he was glad.

'Indeed I'll stay, if you'll have me. Having endured the rigours of your mountain road once, I mean to make it worth while before I face it again. I promised Lucia that I would leave well before the snow makes it impassable, of course. She can't spare me all winter, she says. But until then I am your grateful guest. So, when do I meet Cristabel and this disastrous husband of hers?'

'I thought, quite informally, a reception tonight?'

'Admirable. And the less said about anything, the better. Oh, by the way, we passed another carriage on the long pull up from Lake Constance. I caught a glimpse of its occupants, a pair of old admirers of yours and Cristabel's.'

'Not Lodge and Playfair?'

'I thought you might not quite like it.'

'I most certainly do not. Birds of ill omen! What conspiratorial brew are they stirring now, I wonder? They nearly wrecked Franz's plans last year, with their bungling. I sometimes wondered, afterwards, if they could be quite such inept plotters as they seemed, but Franz would never believe me. I think, if you will excuse me, I had better find out where they are staying. I wouldn't like to think they were planning to pay a visit to Prince Gustav.'

'He's allowed to keep his own court at Gustavsberg?'

'Yes, rather against my instincts, to tell you the truth. It seems to me that one can carry magnanimity too far.'

'And the bastard boy?'

'With his father. And the countess, his mother, and all the sisters. All thriving they say.' A rueful glance down at her own neat waist. 'I'm a great disappointment to everyone, I'm afraid. It's good of you not to have asked.'

'It's not a year yet. Early days to be fretting, Lucia says. But I am keeping you from your business. May I make a suggestion?'

'Please.'

'Why not invite Lodge and Playfair to your reception? I

25

saw them; they must have seen me; it would make perfect sense.'

'Thank you.' With her warmest smile. 'I can't tell you how I hate to play the spy.'

After she had given her instructions, she sat for a long time gazing out at the darkening view of mountain and forest and empty road, while she probed at the failed heart of her marriage. What had gone wrong between her and Franz? Tears throbbed behind her eyes as she remembered the perfect happiness of that public onstage engagement, the glowing promise of their first kiss in front of all Lissenberg. After that it had been nothing but business, discussion, arrangements, and at last wedding and crowning all in one day. And, at the end of it, ceremonial bedding by the whole court – a barbarous custom no daughter of hers should ever endure. But what chance of a daughter – she came to the heart of the matter – when she was still a virgin. Her fault? His? What went wrong? How should she know, who knew so little? And what use thinking of 'fault'? If Franz would only discuss it, with her, with anyone. But, among so much success, it must be specially hard to admit, even to himself, to such a failure. She had hoped that time would take care of it; had practised small enticements, a new dress, a glass of mulled wine in their bedroom, other things she did not care to remember. All to no avail. Did he notice her trying? She could not be sure, but felt the mounting desperation in him, making everything worse. She thought he was glad to go away now, on affairs of state, and pay her the empty compliment of leaving her behind to rule in his place. Suddenly, desperately, she wished Lucia Aldini had come. Had it been, really, on her own account that she had invited her? You could talk to Lucia about anything and in her lazy, relaxed way, she would have helped.

More water under another bridge. She rang for Anna and began to prepare for the evening's reception.

'So Tafur has come to look me over! And we must trail up to the palace instead of rehearsing tonight for tomorrow's command performance. Franzosi won't be best pleased.' Desmond joined Cristabel at the looking glass where she was adding just a touch of rouge. 'That's right. A little more, I think. We must

26

put out all our flags for the old man. Mustn't have him take a poor report of you back to your mama.'

'Old man? I doubt you'll think him that when you meet him.' Cristabel was surprised how little she was looking forward to introducing her husband to Count Tafur.

'Then he must carry his years very well. He was quite in his dotage, by all reports, when I was last in Venice, and that was some time ago.'

'Before we were there.' Cristabel remembered that Desmond had been a failure at the Fenice Theatre in Venice, his Italian not good enough for those sharp critics.

'Ah, if only I'd been still there when you arrived . . . How happy we would have been in that magical city, you and I . . . To think of those wasted years, when I might have held you in my arms.' He swooped down to embrace her, and she was aware, for the first time, that he smelled, ever so slightly . . . Tobacco? . . . Wine? . . . Garlic? Or all three?

She smiled and pushed him gently away. 'If we had met then, my dear, I doubt if I'd ever have succeeded as a prima donna. You are altogether too distracting. And, now, I must really finish myself, or we will be late.'

'And we must not be late at the palace, or our precise Princess Martha will scold us.'

'And have every right to do so.' There had been something in his tone that she did not quite like.

'Poor lady, yes. She needs all the support she can get just now. Have you noticed that she gets plainer every day, poor creature? I am glad to see you such a faithful friend to her, my beauty. I am sure it makes a great difference in her awkward position.'

'Awkward? What do you mean?'

'You're such an innocent! Do you not listen to any of the talk in the green room? The word there is that everyone now feels the husband is away too often and too long. The Lissenbergers put a bold face on it last year, but not all of them much relish having an American commoner for their princess. What with the upper classes resenting the two of them for upstarts, and his revolutionary followers regretting the president they didn't get, things are on the boil below the surface here. And, now, these rumours that Prince Franz has sold out to Napoleon . . .'

27

'What rumours? I haven't heard any!'

'That's just what I'm saying, my star. That you are such a blessed innocent, people spare you the sharper facts of life. I don't know how you managed to go on before you had me to look out for you. So no one has mentioned to you that there is a lady in the case?'

'A lady? What can you mean?'

'You even know her, I believe. Josephine's niece, Minette de Beauharnais. She's a great beauty these days, a star of the Emperor's court. It's not only politics keeping our prince in Paris. Imagine the contrast, a lady of the court, a beauty, with the world at her fingertips, and our poor, plain, well-meaning princess . . .'

'I don't believe a word of it.' But her hand shook as she fastened the pearls he had given her as a wedding present. She had sometimes thought her husband did not much like her old friend, now she was afraid to recognise that he hated her. It was a relief when a servant announced that Franzosi was below, waiting for them, and she was glad all over again that Martha had invited him too. It meant that the conversation in the carriage on the way up to the palace was confined strictly to general topics and the opera they were to put on next night. Franzosi had chosen his own version of *The Barber of Seville*, and Desmond, who knew himself least successful in comic parts was still vainly trying to persuade him to change his mind. But Franzosi was firm, and she was grateful. If Desmond disliked playing Figaro, the comic barber, she knew herself very much at home as the heroine, Rosina, and wondered, anxiously, if Franzosi was trying to make things easy for her.

'By the way,' he said, as the carriage drew up at the palace gates and servants leapt forward to let down the steps. 'If you should be asked to sing tonight, signora, you have my orders to refuse.'

'Orders?' Desmond took it up, bristling.

'Advice then. Lady Cristabel is an old friend. I know she won't take it amiss if I urge her to save her strength for Rosina tomorrow night. And I am sure the princess will understand.'

It was still strange for Martha and Cristabel, who had lived so closely together as friends, to meet as princess and employee, a strangeness compounded by the fact that Cristabel was Lady Cristabel, a duke's daughter, and Martha merely the daughter of a self-made American. Kissing now, each thought the other not in the best of looks. 'Here she is at last,' Martha turned to Count Tafur, beside her.

'More beautiful than ever.' But he did not think it true. 'And the fortunate husband. We are all to congratulate you, Mr Fylde.'

'The luckiest dog in the world, and I know it. You must render my thanks, count, to the Signora Aldini, when you return to her. She will be missing you sadly, I am sure.'

Something in his tone made Martha want to hit him, but Tafur merely turned to Cristabel. 'Your mother sends all kinds of idle, loving messages,' he told her. 'She says she longs to hear you, now you are a prima donna, but you must indulge her by coming to Venice. I am charged with a carte blanche from the Fenice Theatre, by the way. They want to know if you have considered an Italian version of *Crusader Prince*, which we are all agog to hear.'

'Last year's triumph!' Fylde spoke before his wife could. 'Dead as mutton now, count. And untranslatable, you can take my word for that. German opera and Italian are oil and vinegar: won't mix, a waste of time. And if Lady Cristabel were to think of Italy, it would be La Scala, not the little Fenice.'

'You have had an offer from La Scala? The two of you?' Tafur sounded merely curious, interested. 'I'm delighted to hear it. You must have made great progress with your Italian, since last you were in Venice, Mr Fylde. How very wise of you. You're entirely right, of course,' he went on smoothly. 'Now it is the capital of Napoleon's Italy, Milan is very much the place to be heard. I can only rejoice with you, and promise that I will do my utmost to bring your lazy mother there to hear you, Cristabel.'

'But we haven't – ' Cristabel was blushing savagely. 'Desmond is just talking possibilities . . . It's good of the Fenice, but, truly, I want to stay here for a while, establish myself, find my feet. Besides, I owe it to Martha . . . to the princess.' Her colour was higher than ever.

'No, no – ' Reaching out a loving hand to clasp Cristabel's,

Martha was glad of a distraction: 'Here are some old friends. Mr Lodge, Mr Playfair, welcome to our court. I am so glad my messenger found you.'

'You'll always find Lodge and Playfair at the town's best inn.' Playfair bent to kiss her hand. 'We are happy to find you so well established, highness, and only sad not to see our old friend the prince at your side.'

'He will be sorry too,' she said automatically. 'But I expect him any day. Now you are here, you will surely stay a while?' It was the nearest she felt she could get to asking them what their business was in Lissenberg. After they had so signally failed as allies to Franz in the early stages of his revolution, they had turned up, like bad pennies, to represent Austrian interests at the celebrations of Gustav's twenty-fifth anniversary as Prince of Lissenberg that had ended in his downfall.

'With your good leave, we certainly hope to,' said Lodge. 'As a fellow American, I long to cheer at the anniversary of your coronation, princess.'

'And to visit old friends,' said Playfair, 'celebrating the freedom you and your husband have brought to lucky Lissenberg.'

'And to enjoy the hunting, if it is permitted,' chimed in Lodge.

'Permitted?' Martha looked him up and down. 'An odd word, in our free country, surely? But it's true, you will find things changed here, gentlemen. You will be free to hunt, just as all the Lissenbergers now are. It was one of my husband's first reforms, to throw the forests open to the people.'

'With rather drastic effects on the supply of game, unless we were gravely misinformed,' said Playfair. 'When my friend spoke of permission, highness, he had in mind the area around Gustavsberg, where, we understand, the game is still preserved.'

'I see.' What a fool they must think her. 'Yes, my husband has reserved the hunting round Gustavsberg for his father and his little court. You will have to apply to Prince Gustav for leave to hunt there.'

'But we have your permission to do so?' asked Lodge.

'Of course.' It was what Franz would have said.

3

'I never thought of those two young men as passionate hunts-men,' said Tafur to Martha over a late breakfast next morning.

'I'm quite sure they are not.' They were eating alone in her comfortable, chintz-hung private parlour. 'It's an excuse to see Prince Gustav. I wish Franz would get home. Cristabel brought a letter for him from his brother, and I am beginning to wonder if I ought not to have opened it.'

'Prince Max is in Vienna still? And Lodge and Playfair have acted as Austrian trouble-stirrers before now.'

'You think that too?'

'I know it, my dear. I've had it in mind to apologise to you for introducing them as your cicisbeos, back in Venice. That was before I knew, you understand. But we soon began to suspect that they were in Venice to infiltrate the revolutionary movement there, destroy it from within.'

'Just what they tried to do here in Lissenberg. And then they turned up, bold as brass, as Austrian representatives at the anniversary opera. I happened to notice their faces while Franz was being acclaimed. It was not what they had expected at all. And they left first thing the next day, I remember it well. We said "good riddance", Franz and I. He won't be pleased to find them back here.'

'Trying to get in touch with his father. No. I think maybe you should open Prince Max's letter, my dear, though I do see that it is awkward for you. But I take it your husband left you with absolute powers?'

'Of course. He trusts me.' It was true, but had she managed to keep her voice quite steady?

'Naturally. And he will see, as you must, that this new alliance of Austria and Russia against Napoleon changes everything. I confess I am surprised that news of it has not brought the prince hurrying home.'

'New alliance? What new alliance?'

'You haven't heard? Signed back in August. There were rumours, when I left Venice, of a campaign to be mounted in the Tyrol, rather near home for us all, but nothing certain. The Austrians were still trying to persuade Prussia to join them against Napoleon, and then, of course, there was the question of British subsidies to be negotiated. But you can see why I was surprised not to find your husband here. If it does come to war, and war in this part of the world, you and he will have some hard decisions to take.'

'Couldn't we just sit it out as neutrals?'

'I doubt it, my dear.' He smiled and passed her his empty coffee cup. 'You must know by now that the minerals they mine in Brundt are too important to the cannon-makers.'

'I hate it!' Her hand jerked as she poured his coffee, spilling it into the saucer. 'I can't tell you how I hate it. And so does Franz. He was appalled when he learned. We both were. This whole country lives on death. We export it to the highest bidder. It's horrible, count. I'm sorry.' She was ineffectually dabbing at spilled coffee with a delicate lace handkerchief.

'I'm afraid I agree with you, but I'm glad you know. It's always best to face facts, however unpleasant. But what do you hear from your husband?'

'Nothing since he reached Paris. I have begun to wonder if he thinks it not safe to write. Or even if his letters may be being intercepted. Do you think that idiotic of me?'

'Not in the least, I'm sorry to say. We have to face it that since Fouché became Napoleon's Minister of Police again last year, he has been developing a network of secret agents. I think you also have to recognise that your husband may not have been receiving the letters you have written to him.' He finished his coffee and looked at her across the empty cup. 'Have you heard the rumours, I wonder?'

'Rumours?'

'I very much dislike mentioning them. But as your old friend . . . They have certainly reached Venice, and something Desmond Fylde said last night made me think they must be rife here too.' He put down his cup. 'I don't need to tell you how much I dislike and distrust that man.'

32

'No, you don't. Poor Cristabel . . . But, these rumours, count. Please . . .' He still hesitated.

'You know of course that Napoleon is beginning to think in terms of dynastic alliances.'

'Why, yes. He sent Josephine's niece here, ages ago, Minette de Beauharnais, meaning to marry her to Prince Max. You must have heard about that, because of poor Cristabel. It broke up her relationship with Max.'

'Yes, well.' Had she ever seen Count Tafur ill at ease before? 'As a matter of fact, it is Minette de Beauharnais again. I have to tell you, my dear. No one else will. The word is that Napoleon is urging your husband to divorce you and marry her.'

'What?' She put down her cup with a sharp little click on its saucer. 'He won't do it. Franz.' But he could, if he wanted to, on grounds of non-consummation.

'Of course he won't. I haven't even met him, but I know him, by report, better than that. And we must hope that Napoleon is man enough to recognise an honourable man when he meets him. But he has done it to his brothers, you know. Made them marry.'

'He made Talleyrand marry his mistress.'

'Well, he himself married Josephine all over again, in church, last year, so that she could be crowned Empress of the French. You have to think of him as capable of anything.'

'Yes,' she said. 'But I also know Franz. There are things he wouldn't do.' It was cold comfort to be so sure that he would stand by her even more fiercely because of the central failure of their marriage.

'I wish he would come home,' Tafur said. 'And I think you should read his brother's letter. And what in the world are we going to do about poor Cristabel?'

'Let's see tonight's performance first. I wonder if Lodge and Playfair propose to attend it.'

'Yes, they do, they told me so. Art before sport, they say. They are longing to hear Cristabel once more, now that she is an established diva. They had obviously heard the talk about her. Longing to hear her fail, I think. If only there was something one could do.'

33

'I almost wish now I had not asked for the performance. How I hate all this tittle-tattle rumour!'

'Part of the fierce light that beats upon a throne, I am afraid.'

'I sometimes think I hate that too. Franz and I could have been so happy – ' She stopped, appalled at what she had said. 'Yes?' with some relief, to Anna, who had scratched at the door for admission.

'There's a messenger come, highness, from Prince Max, with apologies for the delay, but he hopes to be here this afternoon.'

'Prince Max? Apologies?'

'I told you you should read his letter,' said Tafur.

'I don't need to now. But I shall have to tell him about Cristabel.'

'I hope that proves the greatest of your problems.'

'Max! It's good to see you.' Prince Maximilian had left Lissenberg right after the wedding the year before and had been hard at work on his opera in Vienna ever since, so it was the first time the two of them had found themselves exploring their new relationship as brother and sister-in-law. It seemed very strange to Martha, and stranger still to be so passionately aware, now, of the likeness to Franz she had never noticed before they were discovered to be twins. This was partly because Max had aged a good deal; new lines on his face echoed the ones a hard life had etched on her husband's. 'But, your opera? *Daughter of Odin*? What of it?'

'A disaster. The first night was last week. The only night. They hardly heard it to the end. I thought it so timely, the German theme, the build-up to a new war against France, maybe an alliance with Prussia . . . They say my music is incomprehensible, worse than Herr van Beethoven's. I'm a failure, Martha. I'm only grateful that Lady Cristabel did not find it possible to play my heroine, as I had hoped, and so is not involved in my disaster. How is she? How did the tour go? I thought her in tremendous voice when I heard her in Vienna this summer.'

'She's married.' There was no easy way to break this.

'Married? I don't believe it!' He had gone very white, the

new lines more sharp-cut than ever. 'Not . . . Not to that Irish tenor?'

'I'm afraid so.' What could she say? 'It happened on the journey back . . . They got separated from the rest of the party . . . He felt he had compromised her.'

'Dear God! And she married him? Madness. There are stories about him in Vienna . . . Why did you allow it?'

'I told you. It happened on the journey. They were man and wife when they got here. What could I do?'

'Something. Anything! No, it's not fair to blame you. I do see that. Ah, poor Cristabel, what a disaster. If only Franz had been here. When do you expect him? I have urgent messages for him.'

'I wish I knew. I've heard nothing since he reached Paris. Oh, Max, I am so sorry about your opera, but I cannot tell you how glad I am that you have come. I'm worried to death about Franz. Count Tafur says our letters are probably being intercepted. There's talk – had you heard – that Napoleon wants him to divorce me and marry Minette de Beauharnais? You're laughing?'

'I'm sorry, but you must see it has its comic side. First me, now Franz. And I don't need to tell you he won't do it, Martha. Do I?'

'Of course not.' She was not going to cry. 'But I'm afraid for him if he refuses. As he will.'

'This needs hard thinking.' He was prowling around the room now, everything else forgotten in the face of his twin's predicament. 'He left you in absolute charge here, I take it?'

'Oh, yes.'

'So I must deliver my message to you, in his absence. The Austrians are mobilising for war; they ask for an undertaking that all Lissenberg's mineral exports this year will come to them and to their allies.'

'An undertaking which, you must see, I cannot give. Not until Franz returns safely. And then it will be his decision.'

'You're right, of course. Don't look so anxious, Martha. Napoleon is not Bluebeard. Franz will be home any day now, with his tale to tell us. And I shall stay until he comes. It's only a few weeks, after all, until the anniversary of your wedding and crowning; he's bound to be here for that.'

'That's what I thought. But, Max, there is another thing. If you are here as Austria's emissary, who do Lodge and Playfair represent?'

'They're here? Those two trouble-makers! On what pretext?'

'For the hunting, they say. We thought, Count Tafur and I, that it must be an excuse to visit your father at Gustavsberg and assumed they had messages for him from Austria.'

'If they have, no one told me about them. And that I find hard to believe. So, no, it must be trouble of their own that they are brewing. Or someone else's. I think I had better pay a visit to my father, much though I dislike the idea. He still has Countess Bemberg and her brood of bastards living there, I suppose.'

'Yes. The boy is thriving, they say.'

'Franz should have locked our father up. I told him so at the time. But what's the use of talking? I'll go tomorrow. I must stay for the opera tonight.'

'Of course you must.' She thought she would spare him her anxieties about Cristabel's voice.

Her good friend Ishmael Brodski came to see her that afternoon, bringing the news of the Austro-Russian alliance. 'I cannot imagine why we have not heard of it sooner. I think you should look to the arrangements at your frontier, highness.'

'Yes, I had been thinking that too. I have not heard from my husband either, since he got to Paris, and that's more than two months ago now.' How strange it was to remember that not much more than a year ago, Ishmael Brodski had been urging her to go back to America with him, marry him there.

'I'm sorry to hear that. You should have let me know. I'll have some enquiries made at once.'

'Thank you.' She knew and respected the network of communication that he and his banker friends the Rothschilds had woven across Europe. 'I have been hoping to see you. It's a long time since you came.'

'Yes. I'm afraid I thought it best to keep away.'

'Best? But why?'

'It's more than time the prince got back, highness. It makes one wonder if Napoleon is detaining him on purpose. I don't much like the feel of things in Brundt, and even in Lissenberg there is beginning to be dangerous talk. Grumbles about petticoat government, I'm afraid. I am sure I don't need to spell it out for you.'

'No, you don't. I've noticed it myself. I'm ashamed to tell you how glad I was to see Prince Max today.'

'Yes, that is good news. We must just hope that he will have a steadying influence on his countrymen, who are an unpredictable lot at the best of times. I have to tell you, highness, that there are some who don't much like the things you have done for their womenfolk. Giving them ideas above their places, they say. Have you seen Frau Schmidt lately?'

'No, I've been missing her as I have you.'

'And I have no doubt she has been staying away for very much the same reasons. Women and Jews are always vulnerable at times of crisis.'

'But Frau Schmidt is Franz's – ' She was going to say grandmother, changed it to foster mother. 'I always thought her position impregnable.' She had a vivid memory, as she said it, of Frau Schmidt angrily dispersing a hostile crowd that had gathered around Ishmael Brodski himself. 'What have I been letting happen?' she asked now.

'Don't blame yourself. I think there has been a very skilful campaign of slander and vilification.'

'Based on Gustavsberg?' She was tempted to tell this good friend about her frightening encounter in the vineyard.

'I'm afraid so. Now, that really was a mistake, if we must talk in terms of blame. To leave Prince Gustav free, that was the cardinal error.'

'I'm afraid I agree with you. But it all seemed such a miracle at the time. That instant, bloodless revolution; everything Franz had worked for fallen into his lap. How could he mark it by a first act of old-fashioned oppression? By imprisoning his own newly discovered father.'

'No thanks to his father he was alive to make the decision.'

'Oh, I know! You don't need to tell me of Prince Gustav's wickedness. He was poisoning his own wife, remember! But

37

he seemed such a broken man that night, publicly disgraced, led away by his own guard, not a scrap of fight left in him.'

'He's a very clever man, Prince Gustav. Never forget that.'

'You mean he was thinking ahead already?'

'I'm sure of it.'

4

Martha's messenger found Cristabel on stage with the whole
company in a last minute rehearsal of Franzosi's *Barber of
Seville*. He was not happy about the way it was going, and
had just stopped Cristabel in mid-aria when the man from
the palace appeared at the back of the house.

'A note for Lady Cristabel? From the princess? Oh very
well,' Franzosi grumbled. 'Things can't go much worse, and
we are interrupted already.' And then, as Cristabel read it
and let out an exclamation, he said, 'What is it? The prince
has come? We can postpone the performance?'

'Yes! No. It's Prince Maximilian. He's just arrived. He will
be coming tonight.'

'Then we had better get back to work. From the beginning,
Lady Cristabel, and your heart in it, please. You have fallen
in love with the handsome stranger and long to know who
he is.'

'She wishes it was her husband.' The voice from somewhere in the thick of the chorus got a furious look from
Franzosi.

Desmond Fylde had indeed suggested, once again, that
morning, that he should change roles with the Lissenberg
tenor who sang Count Almaviva, but had got short shrift
from Franzosi. 'Madness, at this late date, and you know it,
Herr Fylde. If you cannot sing comedy, and Lady Cristabel
decides she cannot sing opposite anyone else but you, we
will just have to think again about the composition of the
company, will we not?'

'He was actually threatening me. Threatening us!' Desmond
had entered Cristabel's dressing-room without knocking.
'What's the matter?' She was sitting gazing into the glass,
tears running down her cheeks.

'Nothing. Everything. He's right to talk of making changes.

How can I face Prince Max tonight? He will hear the difference; he is bound to. Everyone else has.'

'Nonsense. You are imagining things again, my queen.' He moved forward to put masterful hands on her shoulders. 'Oh, yes, you're a little tired, who wouldn't be? Just married, with a whole world of delight opening before you. And to be worked so hard . . . Franzosi's a fool and I've told him so. Of course he should have given you time off. What's the use of talking of the Grassini, the Billington, Mrs Jordan . . . Experienced ladies, all of them, what have they to say to a green girl like you?' He bent to kiss the back of her neck. 'How can you be everything your husband's heart desires, as you are, and queen it on the stage as well? It will pass, my angel. Don't fret, and it will pass. And you'll find yourself a greater singer for it, I promise you. It's but to get over these girlish vapours and I've a remedy for them.' He ran a hand over her breast to reach the little watch she wore round her neck. 'Half an hour to curtain up, and your dresser will be here any minute. What you need is to forget your troubles, relax, think only that you are Rosina, Bartolo's captive ward.' He let go of her and moved away, leaving her still sitting, listless, gazing into the glass. Then, 'Here, drink this. It will put heart into you.'

'What is it?' She took the glass and looked at it thoughtfully.

'A specific of my own, my angel. Handed down, father and son, through a line of Irish princes. For the eve of battle, for the moment of crisis.'

'But I never take anything before I go on. How do I know?' She sniffed at it.

'Because I tell you, my love. Many a first night it has seen me through, and me with the hangover on me like death in the morning.'

'It smells good.' Doubtfully.

'It is good! Here,' he took a sip. 'Our loving cup, my queen. Drink it, and I promise you Prince Maximilian will be on his knees to you in the morning, poor fellow. I only hope he doesn't decide to call me out.'

'Call you out?' She looked at him for a moment in honest surprise.

'Fool of a girl, do you notice nothing? Mad for you, he

40

was. Why do you think he left straight after the wedding last year, but that he couldn't stand it? Seeing me; seeing you; seeing us!'

'But he'd never call you out. He's a prince.'

'And so am I, have you forgotten? Come, drink,' he held the sweet-smelling cordial to her lips.

She had forgotten. No; she had stopped believing it. She was so surprised at this realisation that she drank the sweet brew down.

'Not a failure.' Prince Maximilian summed it up the morning after. 'But you wouldn't call it a resounding success either.'

'Partly the opera itself, don't you think?' Count Tafur and Prince Max had met three years before in Venice and greeted each other like old friends. 'A dull treatment of a not very interesting theme.'

'And suffering from the inevitable comparisons with Mozart's *Figaro*,' said Martha. 'I'm a little puzzled that Franzosi decided to rework that old story.'

'Particularly since his lead tenor is so significantly weak in comic parts,' said Tafur.

'Unless that's the reason,' suggested Max. 'But what in the world has happened to Cristabel? She used to act as well as she sang. Last night, oh – she sang like an angel but she moved like a puppet.'

'She wasn't getting much help in the acting from Fylde,' said Tafur. 'He really is hopeless in comedy, that man. If that is what Franzosi intended to demonstrate, he has succeeded. A problem in such a small company.'

'Yes,' Max agreed. 'It has always been one of Cristabel's outstanding gifts that she is equally brilliant in serious and comic opera. What a disaster if this husband of hers is going to drag her down.'

'What a disaster,' said Martha, and all three were silent for a while.

'I'll call on her, of course, on my way to Gustavsberg,' said Max at last.

'Do, and give her our congratulations. Invite her to dine the day you get back, would you Max? You won't stay long at Gustavsberg?'

'Not a minute longer than I must. And send for me at once, please, if Franz returns.'

'What am I to do about the Austrian ultimatum if he does not come?' And then, before either of them could answer, 'What he would, of course. Reject it. But it would come better from him.'

The last time Prince Max had visited the artists' hostel beside the Lissenberg opera house it had been to smuggle his near-dying stepmother in through the tunnel that led down from the palace. It was strange to remember this now as he was ushered up to the star's apartments. The receiving-room he had known so well when Cristabel shared it with Martha and her aunt had changed slightly but significantly. What was it? Lady Helen's embroidery frame was gone from the corner by the window and there were no piles of books on the tables. And instead of pot pourri, the room smelled faintly of cigars.

'I'm sorry to have kept you waiting.' Cristabel looked exhausted, drained. 'I'm ashamed to confess that I overslept this morning. It's so good to see you, Max.' She held out both hands to him. 'Tell me I wasn't a total disaster as Rosina.'

'Nothing of the kind.' But it fretted him that she had used the word they had. 'You sang it beautifully, as you must know.'

'But I don't. I was so tired . . . I don't seem to remember . . . I'm so glad to see you, Max. I needed to ask someone how it went, and you're the very person.'

'The person for what?' Desmond Fylde appeared behind her in the doorway. 'Greetings, prince. I take it you are come to congratulate our prima donna on the way she shone in that dull piece of work.' He was dressed, Max saw with distaste, in an elaborate velvet frogged coat that, on a woman, would have been described as a négligée. 'We are treating you quite as an old friend, you see.' He must have noticed Max's look. 'These late nights at work are hard on a young couple like us.' He gave Cristabel a Turkish look.

'And I am sorry to disturb you so early,' said Max, very formally, knowing it was nothing of the kind. 'But I am on my way to Gustavsberg.'

'Ah, the wicked prince of the fairy tale. I trust you will find him suitably contrite – and adequately guarded. But, forgive me, I quite forgot that he is also your father.' He turned to Cristabel. 'We must offer Prince Maximilian some refreshment, my queen, if he is off on his travels already. I hope you have been able to comfort the princess, prince, in her husband's mysterious absence. We miss him sadly here. Petticoat rule does not suit these Lissenberg boors. But, shame on us, we are quite forgetting! Your great opera, *Daughter of Odin.* Has it been greeted, in Vienna, with the acclaim I am sure it deserves?'

'I'm afraid not.' Why was Max so sure that Fylde knew already that his opera had failed disastrously? 'My only comfort in my failure,' he turned to Cristabel, 'is that you were not involved in it.'

'Oh, Max, I am sorry! But – I can't believe it. Everyone said you were set for a great success.'

'Everyone was wrong. And, to tell you the truth, Cristabel, I don't quite know what the trouble was – why they hated it so.' Warmed by her sympathy, he hardly noticed that he had used her Christian name, as in the old days when they were childhood friends. But then he had called her Bella. If only Fylde would leave them, he felt sure that Cristabel, who had worked with him so long, was such an old friend, would help him to understand why he had failed so lamentably. But it was brutally evident that Fylde had no intention of leaving them. Why should he? He was Cristabel's husband. Max rose to his feet, civilly refused the offer of refreshment and took his leave.

'Ach, the poor fellow,' said Fylde. 'Let's go back to bed, my queen.'

'Frau Schmidt! It's good to see you at last.' Martha had been sitting alone, drafting and redrafting a reply to the Austrian demand, when the formidable old lady was announced. 'How long have you been in Lissenberg? You should have let me know, come to the opera the other night.'

'Good of you, but I am just this moment arrived.' Frau Schmidt was as ramrod straight as ever, not a white hair out of place. 'I have a message for you, highness. We won't be

43

interrupted?' She took Martha's arm and coaxed her gently towards the window, as far from the door as possible.

'Not unless it's a matter of urgency. But – a message, Frau Schmidt? From – ' She looked at her husband's adoptive grandmother with wild surmise.

'Yes, from Franz. He's at my house, arrived after dark last night. Famished . . . filthy . . . exhausted . . .'

'Franz?' She knew the old lady for the most reliable of witnesses, still could hardly believe her ears. 'I've been so worried about him; not a word for months . . . But, Frau Schmidt . . . Filthy? Exhausted? And – in Brundt?'

'He wants you to come to him, help him. It's an impossible situation. It certainly defeats me. He says no one must know he is here until you and he have decided what's best to do.'

'His brother is here.'

'I heard. Gone to Gustavsberg. Let's hope it keeps Prince Gustav occupied until we get things sorted out. But it's you Franz wants, not his brother.'

'Thank you.' Impossible not to mind that Franz had gone to the old lady first, but she must not let it affect her. 'Why would I be coming to Brundt?' Practical as always, she was applying her mind to the immediate problem.

'I thought of that. There's been an accident in the mines, I am sorry to say. I brought you the news. You decided to pay a royal visit of condolence. A surprise visit. How soon can you leave?'

'It's as urgent as that? Well, of course it is. Returned in secret! I'll give the orders; you can explain on the way. I'd best come alone, had I not? May I stay with you, Frau Schmidt?'

'Of course.'

'Is there anything else I need to know, before I give my orders?'

'I don't think so. A fast carriage, not a state one; I'll have mine follow behind. As it is we are likely to finish the journey in the dark, but that is the least of my worries.'

Half an hour later, they were driving down the hill from the palace to Lissenberg and the road to Brundt. 'You are well served,' said the old lady. 'Franz said you would be quick, but I hardly hoped for this. We should be there not long after nightfall.'

'If we don't lose a wheel. And now, explain. It's Napoleon, of course.'

'Yes. He's kept Franz dangling at his side all summer, first at Paris, then Boulogne, then back in Paris again. You've heard, I have no doubt, about Minette de Beauharnais?'

'Kind friends have told me.'

'I was sure of it. Franz refused even to discuss it, found himself civilly prevented from leaving. One excuse after another . . . He must go with Napoleon to see his invasion fleet, recognise the importance of the alliance he was being offered . . . Then came the news of the Austro-Russian Treaty. Napoleon acted like lightning! Back to Paris, his armies marching at full speed across Europe, insisted that Franz go too, see his might at first hand. They were at Strasbourg a few days ago, met the Imperial Guard there. In the confusion, Franz managed to slip away. He had to pawn everything he had on him to pay for the journey. He came by the secret road, of course. Much quicker.'

'The secret road?'

'You don't know? There's a path across the mountains, north of Brundt, takes you down to a tributary of the Danube. Only an expert mountaineer can manage it, but Franz has walked it many times in the old days when he needed to come and go in secret. That's why he came to me, as nearest. And now, you and he have to think of an explanation, he says, that will not involve a fatal public affront to Napoleon.'

'My goodness, yes, I do see.' It warmed Martha's heart that Franz had had such a good reason for going first to Frau Schmidt in Brundt. 'How many people know he is here?'

'No one but me.' The old lady smiled and patted Martha's hand. 'Don't forget, child, that your husband has a past as a desperate revolutionary. He's had a secret way in and out of my house ever since he was a boy. And a hidden room where he used to hide his firebrand friends when they were in trouble with Prince Gustav in the bad old days. So now he's trying the feel of solitary confinement for himself. I can tell you, he doesn't much like it. He is going to be remarkably pleased to see you!'

'It's all extraordinary,' said Martha. 'But what in the world are we going to do?'

'I am sure you and he will think of something,' said the old lady comfortably. 'And now, if you will excuse me, my dear, I think I will get some sleep. I didn't get much last night, I can tell you, what with feeding the poor man and finding him clothes. He was in a bad state when he arrived. It's snowed early in the mountains this year and I think he'd had a hard time of it, though of course he won't admit it. I imagine he will have slept all day today, so I hope you will find him a little better. But he's going to need some cherishing for a while, I think.'

'Bless you, Frau Schmidt!' Martha reached out a hand to take the old lady's:

'Franz!'

'My dear!' They were in each other's arms, laughing a little, crying a little. 'I've missed you so.' Which of them said it?

'You look worn out.' Martha drew away a little to look at him. 'Thin as a rail! But, thank God, you're here. Will he be very angry?'

'Napoleon? Bound to be, but it will be hard for him to show it, since I was never officially styled a prisoner. We have to think of some way of saving his face for him.'

'Yes, I'd been thinking about that. And it's easy, really. You got to Strasbourg in his train – you can't have been at his side all the time?'

'Oh, no, he had a million things to do, as you can imagine, organising that amazing march across Europe. I was just – watched over.'

'Not closely enough, thank God.' They were sitting side by side now, on the cot bed of the bleak little room where he had been hiding, and it was good beyond anything to feel his arm around her. 'You heard, somehow, a rumour that all was not well here in Lissenberg. Strasbourg's a great place for rumour, they say.'

'Yes, indeed. So, what I did hear was wrong?'

'No problem about that, I'm afraid. Has Frau Schmidt not told you?'

46

'About my father? Yes, a little. He's been stirring things up?'

'I think so. And so does Ishmael Brodski. He came to see me the other day. To warn me.' She told him quickly what Ishmael had said. 'We are neither of us so popular as we were, you and I, but I think what brought you home must have been the rumours about me, don't you? You're laughing?' It was good to hear it.

'You're wonderful, Martha. And you're absolutely right, as usual. You're suggesting that I got anxious about how you were managing here and came hurrying home to your side? Now that is something Napoleon would understand. He does rather think a woman's place is in the bedroom. But why did I come in secret?' He returned to the matter in hand.

'Because it was the quickest way? No pomp, no ceremony, no delays?'

'Yes.' Doubtfully. 'The thing is, I don't much want the secret of the path blown. Now I've watched Napoleon at work, I think he's quite capable of invading us by it. Using it to our disadvantage one way or other. It really is a secret, you see.'

'And might come in useful again some time. Max is here, did Frau Schmidt tell you? He brought an ultimatum from the Austrians.'

'She didn't tell me that.'

'She didn't know. They want all our mineral exports. I take it that's what Napoleon wants too. That's what this is all about.'

'I'm afraid so.'

'I have it, I think!' She had been exploring various possibilities as they talked. 'Did Frau Schmidt tell you about the mine disaster?'

'She said something about it.'

'That's my excuse for being here. I'm going to visit the survivors tomorrow. It will turn out that one of them has no one to look after him. I shall take pity on him, like the soft-hearted female that I am, and take him back with me to the palace for nursing. Heavily bandaged, of course.'

'Head injuries! Yes. That gets me to the palace. And, from there? I can see by your wicked look that you have thought of something.'

47

'Not yet, but I will!'

If she had hoped he would ask her to share his hiding-place for the night, she was to be disappointed. But it was inevitable that she must sleep in Frau Schmidt's luxurious guest bedroom, enjoying the sense of being treated more like a member of the family than visiting royalty. Frau Schmidt had cheerfully taken on next day's arrangements, and reported over an early breakfast that everything was in train. 'The women of Brundt would do more than this for you. They don't forget their friends. It's not only the soup kitchen you set up for the women porters at Lissenberg. Even more than for that, I think they are grateful for the way you tried to get them the vote last year.'

'I failed,' said Martha.

'But you'll try again. They know that too. It may have made you enemies, that stand of yours; I'm afraid it has, but it's solved our problems for us today. You'll see, highness.'

'I wish you would call me Martha.'

'Best not, I think, my dear. A dangerous habit to get into. In fact, I had had it in mind to give you a small scolding while I have the chance, if you will bear with me. . .'

'Of course. What am I doing wrong?'

'You're being too friendly, child. We Lissenbergers are a stiff-necked lot. If we are to be ruled, it must be by someone who behaves like a ruler. You and Franz are each as bad as the other. Hail-fellow-well-met to all your subjects! It won't do, and I wish you would tell Franz when the moment is ripe. It's playing into his father's hands.'

'They'd rather be ruled by a tyrant who fleeces them, and seduces their daughters, and behaves like a prince, than by a democrat who thinks of their best interests and shakes their hands?'

'I'm very much afraid so.' And then, with a smile. 'The men, that is. Not the women, as you are going to see today.'

It was an extraordinary morning. By the time they had finished breakfast, the street outside was thronged with women, calling for their princess. When Martha appeared, she was greeted with enthusiastic cheers, and her carriage had to proceed at a walking pace to accommodate the loving crowd that accompanied it. The houses of the men who had been injured at the mine were equally crowded with women who must be presented to their princess. It was all confusion, devotion, and even Martha was not quite sure which of the heavily shawled women who accompanied her carriage was in fact Franz, nor was she sure when he was whisked away to be wrapped in concealing bandages and smuggled into the coach.

5

Martha had sent a rider ahead to arrange accommodation at the palace for her 'patient', and when the carriage drew up in the courtyard she was glad to see Anna in charge of a group of servants with a carrying chair. 'Not a word now,' she reminded her husband before the door was opened. 'We are afraid the blow to your head may have affected your brain.'

'It has my speech!' He managed to mumble it through the bandages. 'You're sure Anna knows which rooms?'

'I'll make sure.' She had been more shocked than surprised to learn that Prince Gustav's suite of rooms, which she and Franz now occupied, had a secret stair and passageway communicating with another luxurious suite known as the Blue Rooms, in an opposite wing. She had objected, at first, to Franz's suggestion that she have him put there, for ease of communication. 'It must be an open enough secret by now, surely?'

'Perhaps. But not one that you would be expected to know. Or I, for the matter of that.'

Anna clearly knew. 'You want him put in the Blue Suite, highness?' She made it more than a question, as Franz let himself be eased into the carrying chair.

'Yes, Anna, and I want you to look after him there. Come to me, please, as soon as he is settled and, for God's sake, don't touch the bandages or try to get him to talk. It was a terrible blow to the head. The doctors are anxious for his reason. Take good care of him,' she turned to the men who were ready to lift the chair, 'but don't talk to him. He needs absolute rest, the doctor says. Don't even try to put him to bed until I have seen him. Just leave him in the chair.' The patient let out a groan. 'Ah, the poor man! Come and see me as soon as you can, Anna.'

The next problem was a doctor. She and Franz had discussed this the night before and come to no satisfactory conclusion. Much to their relief, Prince Gustav had taken his own doctor to Gustavsberg with him and they had not replaced him, sending to Lissenberg if one of the palace servants was ill. Who could she turn to now? Anyone who examined Franz must recognise him, and for once Frau Schmidt had had no suggestion to offer. And the only person she really trusted in the palace was Anna, who had been her ally back at the hostel the year before. She must wait and talk to her.

In the meantime she busied herself with the messages that had come in while she had been away; only a night, but it seemed much longer. Count Tafur had gone on a sightseeing trip to Brundt and would be away several days; Lodge and Playfair had called to take their leave before going to Gustavsberg; she was happy to have missed them. And an Austrian messenger had arrived asking for Prince Maximilian and been sent on to Gustavsberg. She was sorry not to have seen him, and it reminded her that she must send for Max.

But here at last was Anna, looking both puzzled and anxious. 'Who is it, highness?'

'You don't know?'

'Well.' Doubtfully. 'There's something about him . . . And you taking such care . . . Highness, it's not Prince Maximilian? Prince Gustav hasn't . . . ?' She left the sentence unfinished, hurried on. 'I didn't say anything to the men, of course. Or to him.'

'Thank you, Anna. No. You're close! It's my husband; it's the prince. He's not hurt,' she hurried on to add. 'He came back in secret. To Frau Schmidt. We don't want it known how he got here. We have to work something out. You'll help, won't you?'

'You know I will! Oh, highness, I am so glad he is back safe.'

'So am I! He is going to arrive, officially, tomorrow, but in the meantime where am I to find a doctor to help me? He has to be seen by a doctor tonight or people are bound to suspect something.'

'Yes, I do see that. But they're such gossips, doctors. House to house, a word here, a word there. And anything that happens here at the palace is news. But, of course! How could I be so stupid? The Holy Fathers!'

'The Trappists?' She remembered that she and Franz had received a deputation from this silent order after their coronation the year before. There had been some problem about their land, which Franz had settled in their favour. 'Have they a doctor?'

'Yes, a new young one. They found him at their gate, one morning this spring, soon after the road was open. He was starving, threadbare . . . Never told them where he came from, but of course they took him in, fed him up, and found he was a doctor. A good one, they say. He's not taken the vow of silence, not been admitted to the order, but you know what they are like, highness, those Trappists. They won't gossip.'

'They certainly won't.' They seemed strange enough allies. She had never, herself, quite understood the idea of withdrawing from the world.

'And they are the nearest,' Anna pointed out. 'Except for the hostel doctor, and we certainly don't want him. That's a gossip if ever there was one. You should just hear the things he is saying about Lady Cristabel.' She stopped, shocked at what she had said.

'I would much rather not, Anna.' But ought she to ask what they were? Not now, at all events. She made up her mind. 'Yes, do, please, send for the young doctor, Anna. I'll see him first. It's a chance I think we have to take. If I decide I can't trust him, I'll just have to think of an excuse to send him away again. Take some frivolous female dislike to him, do you think?'

'It would be most unlike you, highness. Mind you,' the shared crisis had taken Anna back to the old confidential terms, 'I sometimes think you might be better loved if you did behave a bit more like a silly woman.' And then, blushing furiously. 'Forgive me; I didn't mean . . .'

'I'm afraid I know just what you mean. I had a scolding from Frau Schmidt yesterday . . . but what are we doing? Gossiping ourselves. Send for the doctor, Anna. Say it's urgent.'

'Any message from the palace is urgent. What about the arrangements for tomorrow?'

'I think they must wait until I have seen the doctor, found out if he will help. Because, if he will, it might solve another problem – how to explain the wounded man's disappearing. We'll send him to the Holy Fathers.'

The monks had established themselves some years before in a ruined farm a little higher up the mountain than the palace. The farm had been too high up and too small to pay its way and when the last owner had died without heirs, it had begun gradually to crumble its way back to nature. When the little group of refugee monks had moved in, no one had come forward to object, and, ten years later, it had been one of Prince Franz's first decisions to legitimise their tenancy. Once again, no one had protested. The little farm was invisible from the road that led over the mountains to Lake Constance, and the silent fathers were only remembered when one of them appeared in Lissenberg market to sell the produce they were now getting from their unfruitful soil, and buy manufactured goods in exchange.

Doctor Joseph arrived late that evening, just when Martha was beginning to give up hope of him. 'Thank you, Anna.' She dismissed her and looked somewhat doubtfully at the tall, cowled figure. Monks were something quite out of her American experience. 'You are a doctor, father?' she asked in German.

'But not a monk, highness.' He corrected her in fluent French. 'Though the fathers allow me to wear their uniform.'

'You're French then?' She wished he would push back the concealing cowl. How could she decide whether she could trust him when all she could see were heavy brows over deep set eyes, a beaky nose and a mouth that looked as if it knew how to laugh.

'No, highness, thank God.' He was not laughing now. 'I'm Swiss, from the Vaud. For what that's worth these days, since the French took us over. My grandfather welcomed them with open arms when they marched in after their revolution. He thought they were bringing us union and democracy at last. And now look at us! Satellites! Tributaries! Their taxes bankrupted us; it killed my grandfather. Forgive me, you don't want to hear all this, highness.'

53

'But you are a doctor?' She found herself oddly in sympathy with this positive young man.

'A good one. So they conscripted me into their army, the damned – forgive me – French. I couldn't stand it; it's not my kind of medicine. I'm a deserter, highness. I told the Fathers; they don't mind. I got away from the army of Italy, made my way north, found asylum here just in time. It's exhausting, being on the run. They've been good to me. Lissenberg has been good to me. You need a doctor, highness, I am entirely at your service.'

'I am going to trust you.' She held out her hand and he took it in a warm and comforting grasp.

'You can, I think.'

'Good.' She liked him the better for the qualified answer, and explained swiftly what she needed him for.

'A lie or two?' He summed it up with a surprisingly Gallic shrug of hooded shoulders. 'Against the French? For Prince Franz? It will be a pleasure, highness. And there is something else I think I can do for you.'

'Oh?' She was liking him more and more.

'I found it just the other day. It's almost enough to make one believe in God.'

'You don't?'

'Forget I said that, highness. You're too easy to talk to. I hadn't realised how much I miss women. The thing is, just the other day I was down in the farmhouse cellar. It's a terrible place. Well, all of it is fairly spartan, they don't go in for comfort, the Holy Fathers, but they've done nothing at all about the cellar. It's dry, but that's about all you can say for it. To tell you the whole truth, which I want to, I was down there in the hopes of finding a forgotten cask of wine. Vain hope! But what I found was more interesting. A tunnel . . . solidly built, old, but the air was clear. It has to come here, to the palace. There's a door at the end, with a grille, into a cellar. I'd know it if I saw it.'

'You mean we could get the prince out that way?' Anna's near recognition had been a warning.

'Yes, while I'm pretending to take him up to the Holy Fathers, you will really be getting him up through the tunnel. I'll bring robes tomorrow early. He'll have no problem in that silent house. Then he can meet you, by the road, come back as if from Lake Constance.'

'Admirable. You're an ally in a thousand! Tell me, before I take you to your "patient". Are you happy with the silent Fathers?'

'Happy? What do you think, highness?'

'I think that if the prince agrees you had better come here as our court doctor.'

Martha was hardly surprised to learn that there was a secret passage down from the Blue Suite to the tunnel that gave winter access between palace and opera house. The honeycomb of secret or semi-secret passages under the mountain had played a powerful part in last year's revolution in Lissenberg, and it was strange and yet somehow logical to be down there now with Franz. They found Doctor Joseph's door easily enough now they knew where to look. It was heavily barred on their side, she was glad to see, and stiff on its hinges when Franz finally got it open. 'At least no one has used it for a long time.' She was hastily unwinding his bandages, which they had kept on as a disguise till the last minute. 'Good God!' The last one came away. 'You've shaved your beard. I like it.'

'I don't. But my grandmother said there was no way I could pass as a woman with it, however hooded and shawled, and she was right, as usual. I'll get used to it, I suppose.'

'It makes you look even more like Max. How strange,' she reached up to kiss him experimentally. 'It feels quite different! But we mustn't be wasting time here. I must go back and see your double off to the Holy Fathers. Dear me, I shall be glad when we have got you officially back here, and you can take charge of things. There's been a new Austrian messenger for Max, by the way, they sent him on to Gustav, and I've sent a man after to ask Max to come back at once.' They quickly confirmed the meeting-place at dusk, on a lonely stretch of the mountain road.

'Why will you be out so late?' he asked.

'Because you sent for me, secretly, having confirmed your suspicions of the guards at the frontier post by Lake Constance. I am delighted to have this pretext to get rid of them. I've been sure for some time that they are in Austrian pay.'

55

'It won't make us popular.'

'That can't be helped.'

'How did I ever manage without you!' This time, he kissed her, long and lovingly. 'I hate to leave you.'

'I know. After so long. And so much we haven't said. But there will be time for all that when you are safe home.'

'Home,' he said. 'Yes, for the first time, this palace feels like that. With you in it. You are my home, Martha. You do know that don't you? Whatever happens, that's always true.'

'I know. I love you too. And now I must go and send Doctor Joseph on his way. Till very soon, my darling.'

'Till very soon.' He kissed the tips of her fingers, reluctantly let go of her hand. 'Be sure to bar the door behind me.' He picked up his lantern and started down the dark passageway. She wanted to call out, to stop him. Why was she so suddenly, so desperately afraid for him? Doctor Joseph had come down the passage the other way in perfect safety. She was imagining things. Just like a woman? And the moment had passed; his lantern was flickering out of sight round a corner. She sighed, picked up her own lantern and returned to the Blue Suite.

After she had seen Doctor Joseph and his bandaged charge on their way, the afternoon seemed endless, but at last it was time to call for the carriage. If only she could take Anna with her, the one person she really trusted, but this would inevitably cause comment. Instead, she must take Deborah, the maid she had brought with her from America, so long ago. Deborah had passed, not very successfully, as her cousin and chaperone in London until she had been replaced in these roles by the formidable Lady Helen. It was a pity poor Deborah was so slow in the uptake, but at least they had a language in common that practically no one at the palace understood.

'It's late.' Deborah had reacted to the luxurious palace life by adopting a slight touch of hypochondria. 'You'll need a heavier shawl, highness.'

'Nonsense, but fetch one for yourself if you like. Only hurry, Deborah.' Again she was plagued by irrational anxiety. Deborah seemed to take for ever fetching the shawl, and when they did start out the sun was low towards the mountains. Franz would have to wait for her, and she was angry with Deborah, with herself, with everything.

She had picked a driver and footmen she thought she could trust, and merely told them to drive her over the mountains to where she could get a last, sunset view of Lake Constance. Strange to remember, two years ago, arriving here that first time for Cristabel to take up her position at the opera house, and Cristabel walking eagerly ahead up the mountain with Prince Max. Poor Cristabel.

They were over the top now and the coachman was holding in his horses for the steep downward slope. She wanted to shout to him to hurry as she listened impatiently to a long tale Deborah was telling her about jealousy among the palace servants. She had neglected Deborah, must try and think of some real occupation for her, must also find a more interesting companion for herself.

But she would have Franz. The coachman eased his horses round a steep bend in the mountain road and there was Lake Constance, brilliant in the last sunshine. But where was Franz? He should have been sitting on the rock that marked a martyr's grave; she was to have pulled the check string, stopped the carriage, recognised him at leisure. She pulled the string anyway, told the coachman she wanted to get out and walk a little to enjoy the view. 'No, Deborah, I know you don't want to join me. Stay in the carriage and keep warm. I'll just go down to the corner; I've been cooped up in the palace all day.'

She made herself walk slowly, not at her usual brisk pace at all. How could she spin out the time until Franz arrived? But was he going to? It was already late. What could have happened to him? It was absolutely impossible that they could have misunderstood each other. There was only one martyr's stone on this road, and he should have been sitting on it. She walked slowly down to the corner and looked around; not a soul in sight, and the first lights showing down by the lake, where the houses were already in shadow. How long could she wait?

She turned back slowly, then, as if on impulse, climbed the little path to the martyr's stone. What could it tell her? Was the grass around it trampled? She thought so. By one person? By more? Impossible to be sure. Had he been waiting for her? What could have happened to him? And what should she do?

57

Back at the carriage, the coachman was lighting the lamps, a mute suggestion that it was more than time they turned back. She made up her mind. One last unavailing look at the rock and she started swiftly back to the coach. 'I think we'll just call in on the Holy Fathers on the way back,' she told the coachman. 'I'd like to make sure the doctor got his patient safely there.' And then, aware of the mute protest from Deborah. 'We won't stay more than a minute or two.'

6

'I must talk to you, mavourneen.' Desmond took Cristabel's arm in an owner's grip as they emerged from rehearsal on to the steps of the opera house.

'You are,' said Cristabel dryly. Did she actually dislike the new batch of Irish endearments he was lavishing on her?

'Ah, but quietly, by ourselves, no interruptions. I've ordered a carriage; we're going for a drive; maybe a mountain walk to put some colour back in those cheeks. Franzosi should be flayed alive for overworking you so, acushla.'

'He wouldn't need to if I was singing better.' She faced it bleakly. 'What am I going to do, Desmond? I'm letting everyone down. It's only days till the anniversary celebrations, and we are heading for disaster.'

'It's a disastrous opera. Franzosi can't write them and won't admit it. Come along, my queen, the carriage awaits you.'

'Now? But I'm tired . . .'

'Of course you're tired; sweating it out all day in that airless opera house . . . You'll feel better up on the mountain.'

Maybe she would. She could hardly feel worse. Once again, Franzosi had produced an opera with a comic part for her husband. He had decided that it would be a compliment to Franz and Max to put on an opera about twins, and had finally abandoned the story of Castor and Pollux, whose high drama would have suited Desmond perfectly, in favour of Shakespeare's *Comedy of Errors*, where the twin heroes were largely comic figures. Desmond was to sing both of them, with a stand-in for the final confrontation, and was making heavy weather of it. And she herself was not finding her part as the wife who could not tell her husband from his twin much easier. She had not read the play when Franzosi told her he was basing his opera on it, and, when she had, it was too late to tell him that she thought his choice in doubtful taste.

59

She had tried, just the same, but he had pooh-poohed her objections. Prince Franz was a man of the theatre himself; naturally he would take the whole thing for the joke it was. She supposed the same would be true of Max, but found herself more unhappy than ever about her part now she knew he would be there to see her in it.

'Dreaming again, my honey?' Desmond put his arm around her as the carriage bumped over a sharp corner of the mountain road, and she got one of the whiffs of him that she was appalled to find increasingly offensive. He had always been point device before their marriage: bathed, and perfumed and elegant as to linen; today, as often now, his shirt was not of the nicest and he gave off a faint, unmistakable odour of garlic, and cigar, and man. He was her husband. Surely she should like it?

'I was thinking about the opera,' she said belatedly, in answer to a surprisingly sharp reminder from his encircling arm. 'I still think we should tell Franzosi it will not do. The prince and Martha have troubles enough without our doing anything to make them look foolish.'

'That's just what I wanted to talk to you about, my rose of sharon.' He pulled the check string sharply. 'We'll stop here and walk. Trees have no ears.' They were on the road that led to the Trappists' farm, and he told the coachman to walk the horses, took her arm and led her up a stony mountain path. 'You've heard the rumours too?'

'One can't avoid them. Oh, they try not to let me, but it's too general, isn't it, too taken for granted. Idiotic of Prince Franz to have stayed away so long.'

'A slap in the face for his bride, and no mistake. Well, poor girl, if I was married to that dumpling, I'd stay away.' He pulled her to him for a long, open-mouthed kiss, and she hoped they were out of sight of the road. 'What a lucky fellow I am.' He let her go at last. 'And I'm not risking you here this winter for anything, my bride of dreams. The only question is whether we tell Franzosi now or let him continue in his fool's paradise until after the anniversary.'

'You can't be serious!' She stopped, pulled away to look at him.

'Never more so, acushla. Don't delude yourself. There's

going to be trouble here in Lissenberg this winter, sure as the leaves fall off the trees. Maybe Prince Franz thinks so too, has decided to stay away and save his skin, leave his wife to face the music. What do you think Prince Max and his father are saying to each other at Gustavsberg today?'

'You can't think they are plotting together! Prince Max would never . . .'

'Because he makes sheep's eyes at you, he must be above suspicion? You're not really such a fool as to believe that, my dove. No, we're getting out of here while the going is good. I've written some friends in Vienna already, and you'd better have a word with that antiquated Romeo, Count Tafur. It's about time he and your mother did something for us. I rather fancy trying out my Italian at La Scala, now Milan is capital of Napoleon's Italy.'

'That's why you have been working so hard at it!'

'Well, naturally, my own. You and I are going to conquer the operatic world together, and more than half that world is Italian.'

'You've been planning all this and never told me?' The full enormity of it was beginning to hit her.

'It's a husband's duty to think for his wife.' He pulled her close again for a kiss she did not want. 'And a wife's to let her husband think for her.'

'Plan for her? I'd like to have been asked for my views.'

'Ah, mavourneen, you've troubles of your own with that problem voice of yours. Franzosi's bad for you, we have to face it. The sooner we get you away from him, the better.'

'Problem voice?' It had begun to worry her that she looked forward so much to the drops Desmond now habitually poured out for her before each performance. He had told her they made her sing better. It worried her even more that she was not sure herself.

'Why do you think your busy friend Princess Martha sent for your mother?' He managed a note of irony on the word princess.

'Sent for her?'

'Well, of course! It sticks out a mile. And she was too idle to come – sent Tafur instead. I look forward to meeting that

61

mother of yours. We'll go first to Venice, I believe, whatever happens.'

'All this without a word to me?' She had a sudden, cold, clear vision of just what her mother would think of her husband.

'I told you, my poppet. I thought you had troubles enough of your own. I think we have to go through with *Night of Errors*. It wouldn't do to get the name of contract breakers, but after that, we are free as air.'

'Only because Prince Franz isn't back to ratify the new contracts.'

'Are you so sure of that? Think a little. Prince Franz left his wife absolute authority. She could sign those contracts whenever she liked – if Franzosi asked her to. I'm afraid he is waiting to see how you sing on the great night, my precious, and that's a game two can play at, as I mean to show him. If you look forward to spending another winter cooped up here in Lissenberg, it's more than I do. I only stayed last year for your sake, my angel, and now I've got you.' The words came out with a little, unmistakable snap of triumph.

She stopped, drew a little away, looked at him, facing for the first time the full realisation of her own hideous mistake. He had got her. By marrying him, she had put herself absolutely into his power, and he was beginning to demonstrate it. She had pretended not to notice that he was drinking more, staying out later. Had he actually been showing her that the days of courtship were over, that this was what their marriage was to be like? Had he ever loved her? She almost asked it but restrained herself. The less she said, now, the better. He had made his point, she must reserve her reply until she had had time to think.

'You're getting cold, my queen.' She was beginning to hate the easy endearments. 'We'd best be getting back to the carriage.' He, too, must have felt that the discussion had gone far enough.

'Yes.' Lifelessly. Then 'What's that?' She heard it again. A groan? A stifled call for help?

'What's what?' He had her arm again, starting her back down the path.

'No! There's someone hurt; there in the thicket. This way!'

'You're imagining things, acushla. I heard nothing.' But

when she took no notice, he followed her perforce along the cattle track that led into the bushes.

It was rough going; briars caught at her skirts, pulled her hair; then, from one moment to the next she was in the forest itself, black, thick-growing fir. 'Where are you?' She called, stopped, listened.

'It will be dark soon,' Desmond protested.

'Be quiet!' She heard it again, close now. 'Thank God!' She pushed aside low-growing branches to see where a man had crawled to hide, flat on his face on the ground. He made the strangled sound again, and she saw the gag round his neck, his hands tied behind his back. The hood of his cassock, pulled back for the gag, showed fair hair. 'It's a monk! Help me, Desmond. Your knife!'

'Here.' He handed it to her reluctantly. 'How do we know it really is a monk? Some quarrel among outlaws, more like. Loose him, and he'll attack us. We should get help.'

'We can't leave him here. Whoever did this might return.' She crept closer to work on the gag, by touch rather than sight. 'I'll have this off you in a moment,' she told the rigid shoulders. 'Don't shout; they might still be close. You can trust us. There!' The last savage knot gave to her clever hands.

'Bless you, Cristabel,' said Prince Franz.

'Dear God! Franz! Hold still, while I free your hands. I'm going to have to use the knife, they're savagely tied.'

'I know,' he said ruefully, and lay still.

'Are you hurt?' she asked as she sawed carefully at the strong cord.

'A blow to the head, nothing more. Caught unawares. What in God's name is going on here in Lissenberg?'

'Later,' she said. 'Don't talk; don't move; I'm afraid of cutting you.'

Even when she had him free and they were struggling back to the path, the curiously awkward silence held. After the first impulsive thanks, he had said nothing to explain, and she had hesitated to ask him.

'Well, here's a rum go.' Desmond plucked burrs from his coat and dropped them on the road. 'Welcome home, highness. Can we offer you a lift in our carriage? And how do you propose to explain your surprise appearance?'

'Footpads,' said Franz. 'Will you oblige me by driving first to the martyr's stone? My wife was to meet me there. It's getting dark; she will be anxious.'

'There's a carriage coming now.' Cristabel's hearing was sharp. 'Look, there are its lights, coming up the hill. What should we do?' Unspoken among them was the possibility that it might be the prince's attackers.

'We must chance it.' Franz answered the silent question and stepped into the road to wave an imperative hand at the carriage as it came lumbering round the corner.

'Oh, thank God,' Martha tumbled out into his arms.

'And that, so far as we are concerned, appears to be that,' said Desmond to Cristabel, back in their carriage. 'We save his life and all we get is a quick thank you, and goodbye. Not a word of explanation! They didn't even ask for a promise of secrecy!'

'Maybe they thought it would be useless,' said Cristabel, and then regretted it.

'The servants, you mean. You're right, of course. No way of stopping their clacking tongues.'

'Not footpads,' said Martha, safe in their room at last.

'No. They ambushed me at the rock. How could they have known?'

'I told no one but Anna and Doctor Joseph. And I didn't tell him where we were to meet. But I suppose someone could have suspected something; kept a look out. Idiotic of me to name such a public meeting-place. They took you from the martyr's stone itself?'

'Yes.' Ruefully. 'Like a sitting duck. There I was, straining my eyes for a sight of your carriage, listening for your wheels. Heard a sound, turned. Too late . . . A blow . . . Then, nothing.'

'Who were they? How did you get away?'

'Gustav's men. I was only unconscious for a moment, managed to pretend lifelessness. They were arguing about how to get me to Gustavsberg. They'd left their carriage hidden on the road to the Trappists' farm, had to carry me across the ridge, didn't much like the job. I made myself as heavy and awkward as possible. At last they put me down, started to argue about waiting till I recovered and they could make me walk it. It was getting darker all the time. While they were hard at it, I managed to roll over, slide away into the bushes. It was rough going. I shan't be a very elegant prince tomorrow!'

'No.' She had been busy bathing his scratches as they talked. 'Cristabel was bleeding too. But, Franz, Gustav's men? You're sure?'

'Yes.'

'Max is there,' she said bleakly. 'He went some days ago. I sent a message, when Frau Schmidt came, summoning him back. What do you think Gustav will do?'

'I doubt he'll let him come. I'm afraid we can only wait and see. You sent to order the arrest of the men at the border?'

'Yes. It's going to cause a lot of talk, I'm afraid.' Her gentle fingers had reached the swelling on his head. 'This must hurt! How long were you unconscious?'

'Only an instant. It's nothing to signify.'

'It's nothing to neglect either.' She had hoped so much from this moment of reunion, but she had also thought about it a good deal. 'You must be bone tired. I'm going to give you a light supper, put you to bed in here and sleep in the dressing-room where I can keep an eye on you. We're both going to need all our strength and all our wits about us in the morning.'

'We certainly are.' He caught the hand that was tending him and kissed it. 'You think of everything. I love you so much, my love. Do you sometimes wish as I do, that we were strolling players, living on your money and my wits?'

'Oh, yes,' she said.

Tongues were still wagging about Franz's return and the arrest of the border guards when Lodge arrived with a message from Prince Gustav. After congratulating Franz on his return, he came straight to the heart of the matter. 'Prince Gustav asks your permission to come and visit you. You and he have things to discuss, he says. I am afraid he means to keep your brother and my friend Playfair at Gustavsberg until he has seen you. Oh, they are comfortable enough but confined to the castle.

I don't think either of them is enjoying it much. I do hope you will see your way to granting your father's request. I wouldn't like to contemplate the consequences if I were to go back without the required permission.'

'Blackmail,' said Prince Franz.

'Your brother, highness, and my friend.'

'Do you know what it is that Prince Gustav wants to discuss?' Martha had joined the private conference on her husband's insistence, much against Lodge's will.

'The future of Lissenberg. What else? The news your brother brought makes a decision more urgent that ever.' He had addressed himself entirely to Franz, ignoring Martha as if she had not spoken.

'And what does he propose for Lissenberg's future?' asked Franz.

'Ah, that he did not choose to tell me. Send for him, prince, I urge you.'

'We must, I think. Don't you?' to Martha.

'Oh, yes. But we won't send Mr Lodge, will we? I hope he will give us the pleasure of entertaining him here at the palace.'

'Prince Gustav doesn't care a fig for my comfort,' said Lodge. 'But I'll be happy to stay, if you wish it, highness.' Once again, this was to Franz. 'I brought a messenger, just in case.'

Prince Gustav arrived next day, and once again Franz insisted that Martha be present at their interview. 'We have no secrets from each other,' he told the man he could not bring himself to look on as his father.

'Admirable, I am sure.' Gustav looked sleek and spruce, younger, Martha thought, than when he had been deposed the year before. 'I am so glad to see that there is no truth in the rumours about you two. You do not intend to yield to Napoleon and marry his niece?' To Franz. 'Forgive the blunt question, but it has bearing on our discussion.'

'I do not,' said Franz.

'Spoken like my son.' He turned to Martha. 'I wonder, my dear, if you would not really prefer to leave us. What I have to say next must be painful to you.'

'I'll stay if Franz wants me,' said Martha.

'I do.'

'Very well then. We're here to consider what the future holds for Lissenberg, the country we all love, at this time of European crisis. France and Austria both want our minerals. We want, as we have always wanted, to stay neutral. We can make Lissenberg rich for years to come if we play our cards right. You've not answered the Austrians, I hope?' he said to Franz.

'I thought we had best wait to hear what you and Max had to say.'

'Wise of you. Maybe we are going to be able to deal together after all, you and I, which is more than I ever had hopes of doing with that hothead, Max. So – we sell to the highest bidder, do we not? Or, just possibly, to the first with ready money. In fact, there are all kinds of possibilities, intelligently handled.'

'You think so?' asked Franz, very quiet.

'Well, of course.'

'And who is this "we"?'

'Why, you and I. I had hoped you had seen the need for a wiser head by now. I am going to come back here to the palace as your father, adviser, friend. It will give you two young people the backing you so visibly need. And, better still, it will give you the heir you begin to seem so significantly to lack.'

'I beg your pardon?' Franz was white now.

'Forgive me.' This time he did include Martha. 'But there does seem to be some small delay in the arrival of the little prince everyone longs for, does there not? While the countess and I, I am happy to tell you, are married at last. You will find her delightful company, I am sure, dear child.' To Martha. 'And she will be able to help you to go on rather better with our stiff-necked Lissenbergers. And there will be little Gustav for everyone to pin their hopes on, until, of course, you decide to oblige us, my dear.'

'Never,' said Franz, through gritted teeth.

'Oh, my dear boy, do pause to think a little. There is a very unfortunate accident waiting to happen to your brother at Gustavsberg. He is getting so tired of being cooped up in the castle, poor lad. When he gets the chance, he will very naturally try to escape, and then, I am afraid, he will be shot by mistake. Taken for a poacher, you know. It was so very good of you to allow me to preserve the game on my own estate, while you threw the rest of the country open to the masses. And got small thanks for it, I'm afraid. An ungrateful lot, our Lissenbergers, as I think you are beginning to find.'

'You wouldn't . . .' Franz looked at his father. 'Yes, I believe you would.'

'We will get on much better, dear boy, if you believe me capable of anything where my own comfort is concerned.'

'I should know by now.' He reached out to take Martha's hand. 'We will have to think about this, my wife and I.'

'Don't think too long, my children, or the accident might happen, by accident, as it were. Remember, I'm not asking much. I don't in the least wish to be Prince of Lissenberg again; I'm very happy as I am. I just want to be back in the centre of things, to feel the strands of power in my hands.'

'And see little Gustav heir of Lissenberg?' asked Martha.

'Purely as a temporary measure.' This time he spoke to her directly. 'As a woman, you will understand that my wife, his mother, has her heart very much set on it. There were some extremely tedious rumours in connection with the boy's birth, with which I will not bore you. His acceptance as heir presumptive would take care of them once and for all.'

'What about Max?' asked Franz.

'Ah, yes – he does present a problem. But he's a soft-hearted young man. Approached in the right way, I do not think he would hold out for long. It's a pity that opera of his was such a fiasco, but I am sure he has his heart set on trying again. I think I have managed to convince him that in fact the failure was a political rather than an artistic one. You haven't endeared poor little Lissenberg to the Austrians much, have you, my boy? They like their diplomacy in velvet gloves, masked, as it were. Now, I've the very ally for us, one that will suit you too, I think.'

'Who's that?'

'Prussia. Frederick William and his minister Haugwitz have refused to join the allies against Napoleon. I've been in correspondence with Count von Haugwitz, a most agreeable man and a friend of Goethe. He's more interested in the Oder than the Rhine, and an old admirer of Napoleon, like you, my boy. Who's to say you are both wrong?'

'It's not something I feel now,' said Franz. 'Let me get this straight, sir. What you are suggesting is that you come back here to the palace, to live, with Countess Bemberg and the children? As our adviser? And we ally ourselves to Prussia and sell our lethal minerals to the highest bidder?'

'And name little Gustav as your heir. I've made sure that Max sees something of him, and of the dear girls. Pity they are too close kin for marriage, but then that poor besotted Max is still wearing the willow for Lady Cristabel, is he not? Is her marriage the disaster they say, and her voice as badly affected? I hope you are going to put on an opera for me while I am enjoying my stay with you, so that I can judge for myself.'

'You are taking altogether too much for granted,' said Franz. 'My wife and I must discuss these drastic proposals of yours. We will talk again tomorrow. I take it we can assume that my brother is safe in the mean time.'

'Oh, I think so,' said Prince Gustav. 'And have I your permission to drop in at the opera house, listen to a rehearsal and have a word with my old friend Lady Cristabel? It would be discourteous not to say a word about her marriage.'

'What are we going to do?' Martha asked. The long day crammed with insincere civilities, was over at last and they were alone in their own rooms.

'God knows.' Franz sat down heavily in a chair and put his hand to his head.

'Your head aches?'

'A little. He said nothing about my scratched face.'

'I noticed that too. Well, it saved us a few lies. What would have happened, do you think, if he had had both you and Max in his power?'

'You would have received a still more drastic demand.'

'This one is drastic enough.'

'Yes, in the way it is made. But,' he was actually smiling, 'the disconcerting thing about it, my darling, is that it seems to me to make a great deal of political sense. I've been racking my brains, all this time I've dangled helpless at Napoleon's heels, for an ally who would help Lissenberg stay neutral, and I'd come up with the same answer as Prince Gustav. Prussia is most certainly the one. She's far enough away, you see. She won't want to swallow us whole, as Austria does. I'd been wondering how to get in touch. Well, now I have my answer. Not that I have ever thought very highly of Lodge and Playfair, but as messengers I suppose they will serve.'

'You think they are in Prussian pay now?'

'Everything points that way, does it not?'

'Yes.' Reluctantly. 'I suppose it does. But – your father and the countess, you cannot seriously mean to bring them here to the palace . . .'

'Frankly, my darling, I don't think Prince Gustav seriously means to come. He would dislike it quite as much as we would. I am sure he will be glad to reach a compromise about that. Specially,' he paused, took her hands, 'if we were to offer to bring up the little boy. Would you mind very much?'

'But he's only a baby! What? A year and a half? Something like that. His mother would never part with him.'

'Oh, my dearest, I think she would. You mustn't make the mistake of judging others by yourself. I think you will find that however much they boast of him, his parents leave little Gustav very much to his servants. And you know the saying: Give me the child for his first seven years and he is mine for life. You'd be a much better mother to him, Martha. Would you do it? For me? For Lissenberg?'

'Of course I would. I'd like to.' So much they were not saying. 'But, what of Max? What would he say?'

'Do you think it's true that he still loves Cristabel?'

'I'm afraid so, poor man. If you had seen his face when I told him of her marriage . . .'

'Then the question of his marrying, having an heir, is remote for the time being. And the first thing is to get him safely away from Gustavsberg.'

'From that accident that's waiting for him.' She shivered. 'Yes, indeed.'

'I love you,' he said. 'Right, then. We invite the whole party here for the anniversary celebration, say we cannot make any final agreement without Max, but begin by inviting little Gustav to live with us.'

70

'And send friendly messages to Prussia at once?' she suggested. 'Will they want our minerals too?'

'Bound to. But they would be using them for defensive purposes, as neutrals. Better, surely?'

'Much better. I wish I trusted Lodge and Playfair. And – you'll think me a fool – '

'Never.' He kissed her hand.

'It's the anniversary opera. It gives me the strangest feel. You remember the last time?'

'I do indeed, since it brought us together against all the odds. You're never superstitious, my darling?' Tender amusement in his voice as if he rather liked the idea.

'Maybe a little. I had the same feeling yesterday, in the tunnel, when we parted. I was afraid . . . and I was right to be, Franz!'

'Just a woman after all, not entirely a heroine.' He pulled her to him. 'Oh, my darling, I have missed you so.'

'And I you!' Her arms went up to clasp him, her whole body melted against his. 'My darling, it's been so long.'

'I've never stopped thinking of you, longing for you, wanting you. We're going to start again, now.' He picked her up, started for the bedroom door. 'Damnation!' He paused at the sound of Anna's unmistakable knock. 'Tell her to go away.'

But, 'Prince Max is here,' said Anna.

7

'They helped me escape,' Max told them. 'I don't understand any of it.'

'Who? Not the Bemberg and her daughters?' Franz poured him a badly needed glass of wine.

'No. They must have been the only people in the place who didn't know. It was the servants. They've banded together against Gustav; he's driven them too far this last year. They told me things . . . Not for your ears, Martha . . . We have to do something about our father, Franz. He's not fit to be in charge of a pigsty. Did you know he was arranging to have me shot "by accident"?'

'Yes, he told us. Thank God you are here safe. Does he know you are?'

'No one knows. I thought the element of surprise might be useful, came by way of the tunnel from the opera house, managed to catch Anna. Only she knows.'

'Admirable. I wonder if we could keep your escape secret until the night of the anniversary opera. Spring it on the audience. I have it! We go along with Gustav's proposal, Martha and I, send for the Bemberg and her children to join in the celebrations, get little Gustav safely into our hands. He's only a baby.' He explained their father's proposal to Max. 'For myself,' he concluded, 'I would like the succession to Lissenberg to be open to popular vote, but I have been forced to recognise that this would be anything but a popular idea. And, Max, Martha thinks Gustav is right about your feeling for Cristabel; that we can't count on you for an heir presumptive.'

'Cristabel is the only woman for me,' said Max. And then, 'Oh, if all else failed, I suppose I would do my duty, find some poor willing girl and make the best of things, but why should I? Don't tell me you have let yourselves be influenced by the malicious gossip our father has been spreading! I thought you had more sense. You two have only been married for a year, for goodness sake!' He hurried on, aware that for once Martha was blushing furiously. 'As for little Gustav, I was surprised to find myself increasingly convinced that he is in fact our father's son. I know we all thought it improbable that he could father such a healthy child, but – forgive me, Martha – we have to remember the difference between poor Princess Amelia, daughter of a thousand cousins, and that strapping country wench, the Bemberg.'

'Is that all she was?' asked Martha, fascinated.

'Oh, yes, an innkeeper's daughter. Not so much as a quarter of a quartering to her name.'

'Very much like me,' said Martha, and it was his turn to blush. 'The question is,' she turned to practicalities. 'Do we trust Doctor Joseph, or was he involved in the attack on you, Franz?'

'I'm sure he wasn't. Yes, we trust him. I can see we have been thinking along the same lines, as usual, you and I. So, we send Max to rusticate among the Holy Fathers for a few days, spring him on the audience at *Night of Errors*.' He laughed. 'When you come right down to it, I suppose our opera audience is about the nearest thing we have got to a parliament since they turned down our proposal for universal suffrage last year.'

'A mad idea,' said Max. 'They're not ready for it, our Lissenbergers. You are really serious in suggesting you and Martha bring up little Gustav? I wonder what the world will think of that. Too quixotic by a half, if you ask me. Though it's true his parents don't take much interest in him.'

'That's what I had imagined,' said Franz. 'Of course he'll be better off with Martha.'

'And you don't mind?' Max asked Martha with the directness of an old friend.

'No, I'd like it.' This was horribly difficult ground. What Franz chose to tell his brother about their relationship was most entirely his own affair. 'I just find it hard to believe Countess Bemberg won't object. And, another thing, surely she'll know of your escape by now, Max, and have sent word to Prince Gustav?'

'Not necessarily. The servants who helped me escape will say nothing. And my disappearance will be a puzzle to them. They may wonder if the accident hasn't quietly happened to me, if I'm not tidily dead. No, they'll keep their mouths shut.'

'Of course! Stupid of me. I am so very glad you are not, Max!' She turned back to her husband. 'But what I don't quite see is what it is you mean to put to the opera audience conveniently assembled for the anniversary?'

'Our plans for the succession. It's the best way to put an end to the malicious gossip Max speaks of. We tell them that until we have an heir of our own, little Gustav is to be brought up to succeed Max, if he too continues heirless.'

'Put like that,' said Martha, 'it sounds totally reasonable.'

'If one accepts that little Gustav is the prince's son,' said Max.

'Well, anyway, really,' said Franz. 'So long as Martha has the rearing of him.'

'Thank you.' She was actually near to tears.

'And now,' he went on, 'I think I had better take you along to the Holy Fathers, Max, get you settled there, and for God's sake, no sneaking out for any purpose whatsoever.'

'Not even to eavesdrop on the dress rehearsal,' said Max gloomily. 'You're right of course, but I do painfully long to hear if such terrible things have happened to Cristabel's voice as the unloving Bemberg suggested.'

'The rumours have reached Gustavsberg?' asked Martha.

'If they didn't start there. That's what I have been wanting to find out, whether there's any truth in them, and the only way is to hear her sing. Poor Cristabel. Have you heard her yet, Franz?'

'No. But you're right, I must. Not a command performance, do you think?' to Martha. 'It would fly in the face of all reason so close to the anniversary night. I'd best just drop in at the next rehearsal, as incognito as I can manage it.'

'I wish you would,' said Martha. 'It's not really her singing; there's something very strange about her these days, something I do not at all understand.'

'You think she is beginning to recognise what an appalling mistake she has made?' asked Franz bluntly.

'No, it's not that. Or not just that. When she sang Rosina the other night – oh, she sang it beautifully, a wonderful relaxed voice, superb in all those trills and flourishes Franzosi puts in. But she wasn't acting at all!'

'Can you blame her, with that stick Desmond Fylde as Figaro?'

'But you'd have thought she'd put everything into it, try and woo some acting out of him. You know what a brilliant, instinctive actress she has always been, how the audience yields itself to her. It just wasn't happening. That's when I started to be really worried.'

'I'll take you up to the Fathers, Max.' Franz made up his mind. 'And then go straight back down the tunnel to the opera house.'

'I wish I could come too,' said Max.

'You know you must not. But I promise I'll let you know what I find.'

'How will you achieve your incognito?' asked Max.

'Easy enough. No one outside the palace has seen me clean shaven. I'll borrow one of the Fathers' robes when I'm up there. They refuse to come to the performances, but I've seen them standing at the back of open rehearsals often enough.'

'Do be careful,' said Martha. 'Both of you. I'm ashamed to feel so full of nerves, but I do. I shan't have a quiet moment until this anniversary performance is safely over.'

'You'll be too busy to worry,' said her husband bracingly. 'You must see, my darling, that your job is to keep Prince Gustav occupied.'

'Oh, dear,' she said. 'He won't like that much. And nor shall I. But I'll do my best.'

'I know you will.'

'Nobody recognised me.' Franz returned from the opera house while Martha was changing for dinner. 'Or if they did they kept very quiet about it. But, Martha, there is something very gravely wrong with Cristabel. She's singing like an angel and moving like an automaton. She used to hold an audience in the hollow of her hand. It's gone. There's no heart to her; a brilliant technical performance, nothing more. I had thought – hoped in a way – that the trouble everyone spoke of was some kind of breathing difficulty like the one she was having when we first met. Do you remember?'

'Of course I do!' Lovingly. 'I'll never forget how you bullied us all while you were retraining her voice. Of course I'd been hoping just the same thing, counting on you to put your finger on the trouble when you got back. But it's not that?'

'No. As I say, technically I've never heard her in such good form, but it's like listening to a mechanical doll.'

'Oh, poor Cristabel! How unhappy she must be.'

'I'm not even sure of that. I've sung with her, remember, when we were rehearsing *Crusader Prince*, before Desmond Fylde arrived.'

'I wish to God he never had!'

'That's just what I mean. I remember singing with her as one of the most difficult and exciting things I have ever done. I'm not in the same class as her, of course, and we both knew it. She was doing her best to bear with me, but we could all of us feel the tension in her, the impatience, the perfectionism, if you like. She got more out of me than I knew was there. And now – she's calm, Martha. Totally calm, while that husband of hers makes a public fool of himself. He ought not to be allowed anywhere near comedy. I wish I'd come home sooner; I'd never have let Franzosi put on *Night of Errors*. If it's not a disaster, we're all luckier than we deserve.' And then, seeing her face: 'Ah, my darling, don't blame yourself. It would have seemed the worst kind of interference if you had done anything about Franzosi's unlucky choice.'

'That's what I thought. And then, to tell you the truth, I did wonder if he wasn't putting it on just to show Fylde up, and I'm afraid I rather liked the idea. He's such a boor, that man. I can't bear to see Cristabel with him. And the worst of it is, he makes it impossible to see her by herself.'

'I'd wondered about that. I wish Cristabel's mother had come.'

'Oh, so do I,' said Martha from her heart. 'But I'm her friend. It ought to be possible for me to see her alone, ask her what's the matter. May I tell her you watched the rehearsal?'

'Indeed you may. But the first thing is to get her to come to you.'

76

'I shall ask it for my own sake, don't you see? Might I not want to talk to a friend before taking a decision like adopting little Gustav? How could Fylde stop her responding to an appeal like that?'

'Clever,' he said.

The palace messenger arrived first thing next morning when Cristabel and her husband were still in bed. 'Ah, let him wait,' said Fylde. 'They don't own us body and soul, up at the palace, whatever they may think.'

'It's not like that.' Cristabel was sitting up in bed, reading Martha's note. 'She wants my advice, she says. On an urgent matter. I must go to her, Desmond. She's my friend.'

'She's your employer now. And making the position clear. I told you it was time we got away from this petty tyranny. But I suppose for the moment we must do the civil thing. Tell the man we'll come to the palace after rehearsal this afternoon.'

'But she says "alone", Desmond. She wants to talk to me alone.'

'Man and wife is one flesh, my angel. Do I need to remind you of that again?' He silenced her with a kiss that hurt, pulled her down and rolled over on to her. She fought him briefly, savagely; yielded at last to superior force.

Later she heard him send his message to the palace, lay there among tangled bedding, silent, thinking, making herself think, face what was happening to her. The drops Desmond now gave her before rehearsal, what were they doing to her? Why did she long for them so? Were they really improving her singing, as he said? Why did she not remember how the performance had gone? And – she always felt better in the morning, after sleeping them off. Think about that. And about Martha, who said she needed her. And Desmond? His words echoed in her head. 'Man and wife is one flesh.' Whose flesh? She lay very still, very quiet, until Desmond appeared dressed now, impeccable in snowy linen, ready for the palace.

'Time to get up, my queen. Time for rehearsal, my diva, and here am I, your loving husband, with your drops.' He held out the glass she had come to long for.

And she longed for it. The instant calm, the world trans-
formed . . . 'Thank you.' She took it in a hand that trembled.
'You think of everything.' She hurt all over from his ruthless
love-making. Love? Would she be able to move properly on
stage? The drops would make her feel better. What else would
they do to her? 'That's a new way you've tied your cravat,'
she said, saw him glance sideways to the glass, and poured
the longed-for drink into the chamber pot.

Count Tafur returned from his visit to Brundt that day. 'I
stopped at the opera house on the way back,' he told Martha,
after the first greetings. 'Cristabel looks like death. Have they
anyone who could replace her?'

'It's as bad as that?' She told him of her message, and
Fylde's reply. 'So they are both coming up this afternoon.
I'm glad you will be here. You and Franz will have to absorb
his attention, while I carry her off to my room on some female
pretext or other.'

'Unlike you,' he said.

'Female pretexts?' With a laugh. 'Yes, not absolutely my
line, but one might as well use them when necessary. Tell
me, how did things feel in Brundt?'

'I don't know.' Slowly. 'As a stranger it's hard to tell. Too
quiet, perhaps? And a feeling of strangers not being welcome.
I called on both your friends, Frau Schmidt and Herr Brodski.
Two remarkable people. Oddly enough, they both sent you
the same message, though in different words.'

'And that was?'

'Be careful.'

She could not help laughing. 'As if I needed telling. Is the
news of Napoleon's march across Europe public knowledge
now?'

'Yes, and causing very mixed reactions, as you can imagine.
But, to come back to our poor Cristabel. Should I send for her
mother, do you think?'

'As bad as that? Would she come?'

'If I sent for her, she'd come.'

'But should we ask it of her?'

'That's the question, isn't it? Or rather, the question to
be faced is, what could she do if she did come? Maybe

78

for Cristabel's sake, we should wish Napoleon success in his campaign?'

'Why?'

'You didn't know? French law still allows divorce. Napoleon's new civil code didn't affect that though I'm afraid it puts a married woman's property firmly back into her husband's control. Naturally, we discussed this whole question, Lucia and I, when you sent us the news of Cristabel's disastrous marriage. Normally, we would have settled something on her, given her a dowry, but what is the use when it would merely make her more valuable to Fylde?'

'You're right, of course. She has nothing of her own. Only her genius.'

'I wonder if Fylde knew that.'

'Very likely not,' she thought about it, 'since her aunt, Lady Helen, contributed her income to our expenses. So, you mean the best hope for Cristabel might be a horrible failure in *Night of Errors*?'

'Whereupon her husband would abandon her to her fate. Yes, I do think so.'

'Does Cristabel, do you think? Is she doing it on purpose?'

'No,' he said. 'She wouldn't. You ought to know that.'

'Yes, I think I do, really. Oh, well, what's the use of talking? I count on you and Franz to take care of the wretched man when they come. It's more than time Cristabel and I talked.'

But the first greetings were hardly over that afternoon when they heard the stir of an arrival in the castle yard and Baron Hals appeared, flustered, with a guest hard on his heels. 'All the people I wished to see,' Lady Helen swept them with one of her aristocrat's glances, paused for a dubious moment on Fylde then focused on Cristabel. 'You don't look well, child, what have you been doing with yourself? Never mind; I've news which will please you. I have contrived to persuade your father to make you the allowance he should. I thought the christening of his heir was the time to do it.' Her bright, triumphant glance swept the silent circle. 'What's the matter? What's going on here?'

Desmond Fylde took a step forward. 'I must be the first to

thank your ladyship.' He took and kissed her reluctant hand. 'On my wife's behalf as well as my own.'

'Your – ' She look at him in blank horror, turned to Cristabel, 'His? . . . No wonder – ' She stopped. 'I do not feel quite the thing,' she said at last turning to Martha. 'Forgive me, highness, for this abrupt intrusion. With your permission, I'll take my leave. Cristabel will see me back to the hostel.' She swept past Fylde as if he did not exist, took Cristabel's arm and left the room with her.

'Well, I'll be – ' Fylde looked about him, reconsidered, and followed them.

'She has had the carriage door shut in his face,' said Tafur, from the window. He turned to Martha. 'Perhaps I do not need to send for Lucia after all.'

'No,' said Martha. 'But what a disaster.'

'The allowance, you mean. Yes, poor Lady Helen, one does have to feel sorry for her.'

'And for Cristabel,' said Martha.

'But she has a gained a redoubtable ally. I am not sure it is not Fylde we should start pitying.'

'Never,' said Martha.

8

'It's a complete disaster.' Lady Helen had called at the palace next day and found Martha alone. 'You cannot possibly blame me more than I blame myself. But the invitation came so unexpectedly and at such short notice. It seemed the perfect chance to talk sense into my brother; I never for a moment imagined Fylde would be capable of such wickedness.'

'Or such planning,' agreed Martha ruefully. 'But, Lady Helen, what does Cristabel say? Were you able to talk to her? He's been making it impossible . . .'

'She's in a very strange state,' said Lady Helen. 'There's more wrong with her than mere unhappiness, I think, though she is unhappy enough, poor child. She is in a terrible fret about the performance next week. She talked mostly about that, about her voice. She was shaking, Martha, actually shaking.' And then, recollecting herself: 'Forgive me, highness.'

'Don't,' said Martha. 'I am so very glad you are come. We had been talking of sending for Cristabel's mother, Count Tafur and I, but this is better. Shaking, you say? Should she see a doctor?'

'She won't hear of it. Well, you know the hostel doctor; a gossip if ever there was one, and that is something she most absolutely cannot afford. She's just tired, she says; needs a rest, needs a holiday. She even thanked me for getting her the allowance, says now she and her husband can have some time to themselves, go on a little wedding tour. She said it as if it was a sentence of death. And then we were at the hostel, and there were all the arrangements to be made about my arrival. I had looked forward to it so much! All confusion, disappointment . . . And then he arrived, very angry in a quiet way and I've not had a private word with her since. What are we going to do, Martha?'

'Two things,' said Martha. 'First, I am going to ask Franz

to see to it that there is someone ready to take her part next week, if the worst comes to the worst, to get that load off her mind, though she won't like it. But Franzosi must see the need for this, maybe he has already. And the other thing is to get a doctor to her. And I know the very man.' She described Doctor Joseph without going into the circumstances of their first meeting. 'I've been meaning to invite him to come to the palace as our doctor, specially now that we are thinking of having little Gustav to live with us – ' She silenced Lady Helen with an imperative hand. 'I'll tell you about that some other time. There has been a great deal going on here while you have been away, and I shall be glad of your advice, but for the moment, Cristabel must come first. I shall send Doctor Joseph down to see her, or rather Franz will. He went to a rehearsal the other day, and was shocked at her appearance. He's her employer after all. He has every right to send his own doctor to her.'

'Fylde won't like it.'

'There's nothing he can do about it. Their new contracts haven't been signed. I thought they should wait until Franz returned.'

'Maybe he won't care about that, now that she has the allowance.'

'Oh, no, he'll care. He's an ambitious man, Desmond Fylde, and a greedy one. He'll take the allowance as an agreeable extra, but it won't satisfy him. He's insatiable, I think.'

'I'll never forgive myself.'

'What's done is done. I feel just the same, but what we have to do is think about freeing her.'

'Divorce?' Horrified.

'Her father managed it.'

'He's a duke.'

'You mean, he's a man. Why is everything easier for them?' And then, remembering Franz, 'No, not everything. I don't know how soon I shall manage a word alone with Franz,' she warned Lady Helen. 'He's been so busy since he got back that I almost have to make an appointment to see him. Everyone seems to have saved their problems for him, which is scarcely flattering to me as his substitute.'

'But understandable, I suppose.'

82

'Oh, yes, entirely understandable.' Did she quite manage to keep the note of bitterness out of her voice? 'Specially here in Lissenberg. Lord, I'll be glad when this anniversary is well over and the roads closed and we can settle down for the winter.'

'With Napoleon God knows where? Oh – it's a relief, of course, that the threat of an invasion of England has lifted. There was near panic when I was there, and the mob in the streets shouting for Lord Nelson as if he were all the heroes rolled into one. I heard them myself. I've never been so shocked! Living in open sin with Lady Hamilton as he does. There are even rumours of a child. Tell me, my dear – '

'Better a flawed hero than none,' Martha forestalled her question. 'As to Napoleon, from what Franz says he's more than half way to Vienna by now. I hope the snow comes early this year, and walls us in. It's a great advantage we have, that time of safety.' Would there be time, then, in the long winter nights, for her and Franz? At the moment, he came to bed so late and so exhausted, that her only thought was to let him get enough rest to prepare him for the next day's problems. Should I be more selfish, she wondered, and made herself listen to what Lady Helen was saying.

Prince Max would have found the boredom of life with the Trappist Fathers intolerable if it had not been for the company of Doctor Joseph, who had welcomed him with open arms and a volley of questions about the outside world. They had become firm friends by the time the messenger from the palace found them sitting over a hard fought game of chess. 'Prince Franz wants me to go and see Lady Cristabel?' Doctor Joseph looked surprised. 'What do I know about singers? Or ladies, come to that, specially noble ones!'

'Lady Cristabel is ill! What's the matter?' Max almost snatched the note his new friend handed to him. 'He doesn't say. But it must be serious for him to intervene. You'll go at once? Oh God, I wish I could come with you. She's . . . Poor Cristabel . . . You've heard the talk about her voice of course?'

'A little. And about her marriage. Will the husband be

pleased to see me, do you think?' Doctor Joseph was interested in his new friend's vehement reaction.

'Furious, I should think. He's bound to make it as difficult for you as possible. That's why it is a direct commission from my brother, I'm sure. To smooth the way for you.'

'Yes.' Doubtfully. 'I find it an awkward enough compliment, this commission! But I don't need to leave yet. Tell me about Lady Cristabel, since I can see you are a friend of hers.'

'A friend!' It was almost a groan. 'I love her. Always have, always will. She came to Lissenberg with her father, the Duke of Sarum, when we were children – well, young; for a children's opera, *Orpheus and Euridice*. I was to sing Orpheus, naturally, she was Euridice. She persuaded me to change parts. I loved her. She could have persuaded me to anything. She was . . . I cannot tell you what a miracle she was. The first time on any stage, and she held that audience in the palm of her hand. We were masked, you understand, they all thought it was I. We had intended to keep the masks on, but when it came to the applause, I could not do it. She had to have the glory that was hers. Both our fathers were furious. The duke took her away next day, immured her in his country house. We did not meet again for years. You know the story, I expect. The princess was Martha Peabody then, a rich American's heiress daughter. She fled the American fortune hunters, met Cristabel in England and brought her to Europe to further her career. I met them in Venice, lost my heart all over again, if there was any of it left to lose. They came here, to the opera house. I was biding my time to speak to her, fearing that she might not have remembered me as I had her.' He paused, looking back over the old disaster.

'Yes?' prompted his friend. 'So, what happened?'

'Napoleon! Oh, he was Bonaparte still, but a power to be reckoned with. Thinking dynastic thoughts. He proposed a marriage between me and his wife's niece, Minette de Beauharnais. I held out as long as I could, but – you don't know my father! The threats he used. Franz is wrong to think he can co-operate with him.' He realised this as he remembered the past. 'He's mad; I must tell him, warn him.' He made as if to rise.

'Not instantly!' said his friend. 'You're in hiding, remember,

84

on his orders. Wait until I've seen Lady Cristabel, got a feel of things in town. I'll volunteer to do the Fathers' marketing in Lissenberg,' he explained. 'Might as well, by the time I have been down to the opera house. That way I can pick up all the talk.'

'Not come straight back?' Disappointed.

'You'll have to possess your soul in patience, my poor friend. I may even spend the night in Lissenberg, drop in on a few acquaintances, hear what they have to say, do my errands in the morning. You'll just have to bear it! And don't, I beg you, for everyone's sake, do anything foolish.'

'I won't. I promise. After all, I promised Franz.'

Doctor Joseph rode down the hill to the opera house on the flea-bitten old cavalry horse on which he had arrived in Lissenberg, and Max, watching him go, was amused at the contrast between his monk's attire and his military seat in the saddle.

In his note, Prince Franz had promised to tell Lady Cristabel the doctor was coming and leave it to her whether she chose to see him in her dressing-room at the opera house or at home in the hostel. Calling at the opera house first, Joseph drew a blank. Lady Cristabel had gone home early, the doorkeeper told him, with a knowing look.

At the hostel, as he had expected, he found Desmond Fylde awaiting him in the downstairs reception room. 'Doctor Joseph?' He wasted no time on courtesy. 'My wife can't see you, I'm afraid. She has enough on her mind, with the performance next week, without being troubled by quack physicians.'

'Ah.' Joseph had seen the handsome tenor on stage often enough, but had never been close to him before and his acute eye was busy summing him up as probably ten years older than he looked in costume. Maybe more? No wonder he had decided to set himself up with a wife to support him. He said no more, but put down his instrument case on a table, reached leisurely into an inner pocket and produced a parchment scroll. 'My qualifications, Herr Fylde.'

'Latin!' Fylde looked at him with dislike.

'Paris.' Pointing at the word. 'Seventeen hundred and

ninety-six. I am afraid the date is in Latin numerals. But I can promise you it is all quite in order. Does Lady Cristabel perhaps read Latin?'

'I've no idea.' It was obvious to Joseph that Fylde did not at all want to reveal to his wife that he could not. 'Well,' he said now, grudgingly, 'I suppose that is something. That you are properly qualified at least. But I still don't want my wife troubled. It's all in her mind, you know.' Man to man. 'A case of nervous strain. She thinks she can't sing, then, of course, she can't.'

'Very interesting,' said Joseph. 'And, in fact, rather what I had thought myself from hearing her. I can see that you are a man of perception, Herr Fylde. I wonder how you proposed to convince her that she can, in fact, sing?' And then, as Fylde hesitated, searching for an answer: 'May I venture to suggest that if you were to let me see her, and I was to tell her that it was all in her mind, it might form just the kind of cure you suggest? The word of a medical man, you know? Husbands do tend to be partial judges, she may think you are sparing her feelings, while there is no reason why I should.'

'And you'd do that?'

'If I thought it was best for her. Naturally, I would need to see her, satisfy myself that there is no physical problem. But, frankly, I am convinced there is not. It is a question of medical ethics, you understand. I'd need to see her alone, just a few very simple questions, and then I could give her the reassurance she so badly needs. It would be a tragedy, would it not, if this anniversary performance which should be the cornerstone of her career should mark its end.'

'That's what they are saying?'

'I am afraid so, Herr Fylde. You know how it is, the nearest and dearest are the last to hear this kind of rumour. And, another thing, the expectation so often brings the fact. If the audience arrive convinced that Lady Cristabel is going to fail, the chances are very strong that she will. How sad it would be. Such an immensely promising career, such a future opening before her.'

'A disaster?' Was Fylde facing it for the first time?

'Whereas if I were to see her,' Joseph went on. 'And go down into Lissenberg afterwards, as I mean to, and mention, quite casually, here and there, that I have found out what was the matter and dealt with it. Well, do you know, without flattering myself, I think it might make a difference.'

'Admirable man. She shall see you at once. I was only wanting to make sure that you would not do more harm than good, you understand?'

'Of course I do.' Left alone, Doctor Joseph smiled to himself, rolled up the useful piece of parchment and put it back in his pocket.

Five minutes later Desmond Fylde ushered him assiduously into the big bedroom which showed signs of a rapid tidying. 'This is Doctor Joseph, my dear. I am sure he will do you good.'

'Joseph?' She was sitting on a *chaise longue*, dark hair curling loosely around the pale face, brilliant blue eyes summing him up. 'Joseph what?' The extraordinary eyes moved to see the door close behind her husband.

'Just Doctor Joseph, madame.' He felt as if the blue eyes were penetrating, layer upon layer, through to his naked heart.

'Doctor Joseph.' She said it thoughtfully in French. 'Would you be so good, monsieur, as to put back your hood? I cannot persuade myself to discuss my problems with someone whose face I cannot properly see. Thank you.' Blue eyes met blue eyes for a long moment. 'And now, tell me how you persuaded my husband to let you see me alone.'

'Easy, madame.' The laughter in his eyes somehow communicated itself to hers. 'I blinded him with science and told him I would tell the world you were cured.'

'And shall you?'

'When you are.'

'So easy?'

'I rather hope so. I have been studying you a little, madame. I hope you won't mind this, but it's a dull life up with the Trappist Fathers.'

'And you have enlivened it by studying me? Thank you, monsieur.'

'It's been a pleasure. So – ' His eyes held hers. 'What has he been giving you?'

'You know?' She put a hand to her heart.

87

'I am a doctor, madame. And not a fool.' He took her hand, and felt the shock of it pass through them both. 'You see, it is shaking.' He was holding it professionally, counting her pulse, ignoring the shocks that still ran through him.

'Of course it's shaking. Who are you, monsieur?'

'You are more honest than I am, madame.' He did not answer her question. 'But – it was shaking before. Why was that?'

'Because I stopped taking his drops.' It was the most natural thing in the world to answer him straight.

'What were they?'

'I don't know. He said they were handed down by the princes, his forebears.' Her tone proclaimed her disbelief in them. 'I didn't like what they were doing to me. On stage. I couldn't remember, afterwards, how it had gone. And there was something missing, something wrong . . . I felt wonderful at the time. It's been hard . . .'

'I'm sure. Does he know you have stopped?'

'No. It's only been a couple of days. I've contrived to get rid of them . . . I'm surprised he let you see me, even with Prince Franz behind you.'

'I think I managed to frighten him. Besides,' once again that instinctive, vital exchange of smiles, 'I promised I'd cure you.'

'Cure?'

'Of the affliction of the nerves that is affecting your voice.'

'That's honest, at least. You have heard me then? I thought – ' What in the world had she been thinking?

'That I was a Trappist, vowed to silence and the cloister? No, madame, I am merely a refugee whom the Fathers have charitably taken in. I'm Swiss, conscripted into the French army of Italy – a nobody – worse, a deserter.' He made it a challenge. 'And my exile, here in Lissenberg, has been brightened by listening to you.'

'You've been here some time, then?'

'Since the spring. Long enough to have heard the change – forgive me, the trouble when you came back from your summer tour.'

'I was so tired . . . He said it was just that . . . Gave me the drops . . . They made everything seem easy!'

'And you sang brilliantly,' he told her. 'I've never heard you better, technically.'

'Technically? What are you trying to say?'

'I was at a rehearsal of *Night of Errors* the other day. What a waste of your genius! But never mind that. You had every one of Franzosi's old-fashioned trills and shakes to perfection! And no heart in it, no life, nothing. You could have been a music machine. The audience felt it, of course.'

'That's what it is! What I'm missing. The feel of the audience reacting. Oh, I do thank you for telling me. But what can I do? Without Desmond's drops I can't sing; with them I can't act! Does that sum it up?'

'You're a remarkable woman. How long do you think before he interrupts us?'

'I'm amazed he's not done so already. Have I told you about the drops?'

'Yes, and I've forbidden you to take them. Ah – ' They had both heard the door open. He turned: 'Herr Fylde! And in the nick of time. I've a hard regime to prescribe for your wife, I am afraid. For both of you. If you will forgive us, madame? A word with your husband alone?'

'Oh.' They could both see that she did not like it. Then: 'Very well.' Coolly. 'Goodbye, then, doctor, and thank you.' She held out her hand and he surprised them all by kissing it.

'How old is your wife?' Back in the downstairs receiving room he surprised Fylde with the direct question.

'How old? Twenty-one? Twenty-two? What's that to the purpose?'

'A good deal, I think.' Doctor Joseph's cowl was back in place, and he had shaken his head at Fylde's offer of a glass of wine. 'You are, shall we agree, a good deal older?'

'A few years. Yes?'

'And naturally, much wiser. A man of the world. Responsible for her; anxious about her, as any husband would be. That's why you gave her that family medicament of yours. That extraordinary potion that seems to have done her so much good.'

'Ah. She told you about that?'

'In answer to a question. I have followed her career with

89

great interest, sir. With great admiration. We cannot afford to lose so brilliant a singer.'

'To lose? You cannot think – '

'I think, at the moment, that anything can happen. The musical world owes you a great debt, sir, for having had the wisdom to see the threat to your wife's voice. I respect you for what you have tried to do for her, but I have to tell you that it will not do. There are times when an artist has to work through his (or her) problems without outside assistance. I think this is one of them. I think we must all stand back from Lady Cristabel, if we wish to see her the prima donna of the new century, leave her alone with the great problem of her genius.'

'Leave her alone? What precisely do you mean by that, doctor?'

'You're not a fool, sir. Far from it. You are a man of wide experience. You must see what it has been like for her, suddenly married to a man like you. Overwhelmed by him. Now, you have to think – and for all our sakes, I beg you to think carefully, which you want most: the young bride or the prima donna?'

'Want? What do you mean?' He could not decide whether to be angry.

'I think you know what I mean. Why I asked to speak to you alone. Lady Cristabel has the world before her. In five years she could be choosing between the golden offers of La Scala, the San Carlo . . . Or she could be the happy mother of your children, singing, perhaps, a little between pregnancies.'

'Oh, no, give me credit for a little worldly wisdom, doctor. I've taken thought to that.'

'I'm glad to hear it, but the best-laid plans, you know . . .' Bile was rising in his throat and it was with an effort that he kept his voice steady, light, man to man. 'But there is more to it, just now, is there not? If she is to succeed, as we all hope she will, at this important anniversary performance, she needs her whole heart in her singing. How can it be, with a handsome new husband always at her side?'

'What are you suggesting?'

'I am prescribing a simple regimen of separate rooms until after the performance. I am sure there is some charming young creature in the chorus whose heart was broken when you married. Yes, I see there is.' He made himself respond to Fylde's smirk. 'And no more drops, Herr Fylde. This is a battle Lady Cristabel has to win by herself. Once she is firmly established as the diva we know, then, what a happy reunion!' It made him sick to suggest it, and in these vulgar, man-to-man terms, but the extraordinary thing was that everything he had been saying was perfectly true.

'She will mind it,' said Fylde preening himself. 'How do I explain it to her?'

'Why, blame it on me, of course!' Would she mind it? Could he bear to think about this? What in the name of God was happening to him?

'You don't think you should see her again, explain?'

Here was temptation, flaming, outrageous temptation. Its very strength told him it must be resisted. 'No, that is the husband's part, Herr Fylde. You have taken on a heavy responsibility in marrying so brilliant a young creature. I feel for you, and will help you in every way I can but that. But I will come again, if I may, after I have next heard her sing. To encourage her, tell her how much better she is singing.'

'Suppose she's not?'

'I'll suppose no such thing.'

9

After a fruitful evening in Lissenberg, Doctor Joseph dropped in to the rehearsal at the opera house next morning, his monk's habit, as always, his passport. He arrived to a buzz of excitement. Cristabel and Fylde were alone on stage, Franzosi haranguing them. The chorus members, sitting in the front rows, were alive as if with electricity. 'What's happened?' Joseph whispered to the man next to him. 'What's going on?'

'It's the diva! Our heroine, Adriana. Wait till you hear her! She's herself again, or nearly. If only the opera was better! And she's showing up Fylde as the old ham he is. I wonder how he likes that. Hush!'

Cristabel was on the upper stage now, supposedly looking out of her bedroom window, summoning the wrong twin, the man she thought to be her husband to come in to her: 'Where have you been, my darling, this long day?' The music was trite enough, but she was putting such passion into it that Joseph whispered: 'It might be Gluck or Handel.'

'Franzosi's in a dream of glory.' The man recognised him. 'You're the doctor, aren't you? We all owe you a great debt. I thought – We were all afraid we had a disaster on our hands. Can she keep it up, do you think?'

'I don't see why not.' He was wondering whether to call at the palace, decided to let the good news find its own way there. Besides, he thought he might indulge himself in a moment with her. Extraordinary to have one's whole life reorient itself in one ten-minute interview – in one minute. As to what would come of it? Time enough for that.

'I'm not surprised you look so happy, you deserve to.' The chorus member had risen to his feet at a summons from Franzosi.

'Do me a kindness, friend?'

'Gladly.'

'Tell her I'm here and would like to congratulate her. When she can.'

'Delighted, I'm sure.'

He saw the message given and received, saw the quick movement of her head as she searched the darkened house for him, waited with hard patience as Franzosi tried to coach Fylde into the comedy of his scene of misunderstanding with her. Since he played both her husband and his twin, there was no question about the likeness that betrayed her into mistaking a complete stranger for her husband. It should have been exquisitely comic, failed hopelessly because of Fylde's inept acting. In the end, Franzosi let out an almost audible sigh and changed his tack. Fascinated, Joseph watched as he let Fylde have his head, betray himself for the boor he was. If it was not the interpretation of his opera Franzosi had intended, it might still be a brilliantly successful one. At Fylde's expense.

'I do thank you.' She was there at his side, and he had actually not felt her come.

'I congratulate *you*.' He reached out, took her hand, felt yesterday's amazing message renew itself.

'I sang it for you,' she said, as if it was the most natural thing in the world. 'And then you were there.'

'I hope I shall always be there.'

'But how? What are we going to do?'

'Nothing, until after next week's performance.' He had pulled her gently down to sit beside him, and the nearness was intoxicating. 'Trust me?'

'I do. It's mad.' Were they both remembering that she had trusted Fylde?

'Do, just the same. You can. To the end of the world, and you know it. As I do you. He's leaving you alone?' He had to ask it. And then: 'You're trembling!'

'With laughter. I'm ashamed, though. Have you seen the seconda donna's face this morning? Torn between triumph and tears. Franzosi had asked her to be ready to take my place. Oh, nobody told me, but I knew. And quite right too,' she went on. 'I know that. Poor thing. She should have been learning her words last night. Instead – ' she paused for a moment, 'Desmond made me a great matrimonial scene of renunciation after you left. Your doing, and I thank you. My career must come first . . . My debt to the world . . . Tell me, how could I have been such a fool? Have you seen what he is letting Franzosi do to him?'

'Yes. What are you going to do about it?'

'Nothing. What can I? I owe him nothing.'

'Less than nothing. So, he spent the night with the seconda donna.' He said it for her.

'I should be furious.'

'And you're relieved. Good. As your doctor, I can only congratulate you. You will send for me if you find you need my services again.' His tone warned her, and she turned to see her husband at her side.

'I've been thanking Doctor Joseph,' she told him.

'So must we all.'

On Franz's suggestion, Prince Gustav had gone himself to bring his family to the anniversary celebration, and Martha was busy arranging the most remote of the palace's guest wings for their reception. Tension crackled in the air. There had been no news from the outside world for some time, but reports from the opera house were increasingly cheering. Cristabel was singing better than ever, everyone said, more than making up for Fylde's shortcomings. Martha longed to thank Doctor Joseph for the part she was sure he had played in Cristabel's recovery but when she invited him to the palace, to discuss this and her suggestion that he become their doctor, he sent a civil refusal, explaining that he felt he should stay with Prince Maximilian until after the anniversary performance. Max must be getting restive.

When she told Franz about this, in one of their rare moments alone, he laughed. 'What a bold little doctor,' he said. 'To refuse a princess. There's something about that man,' he went on thoughtfully. 'I wish I knew what it was. Lord, I'll be glad when this celebration is over.'

'And winter comes,' she said. 'And the quiet.' It was a kind of promise between them.

It had been Franz's decision that the celebration of the first anniversary of his reign should be a quiet, domestic one and

Martha had wondered, from time to time, whether he had been right. A leaven of outsiders might have eased what promised to be an awkward enough occasion. And now Prince Gustav had stipulated that the Countess Bemberg be recognised as his wife, Princess Gertrude, and there had seemed nothing for it but to agree. 'I doubt the Lissenbergers will like it much,' Martha told Franz.

'I don't pretend to know what they like or don't like any more. Something's going on, I don't know what.' He looked increasingly hag-ridden, she thought. 'I seem to be out of touch since I got back. Madness to stay away so long, but how could I help it?'

'You can hardly announce now that Napoleon was keeping you against your will.'

'No, that would be to negate all the trouble we have taken not to make a diplomatic issue of it. But I tell you, I like the feel of things less and less. What does Ishmael Brodski say?'

'He's worried too. He's not coming to the performance, says he thinks it's a time for him to lie low. But Frau Schmidt is coming, bless her.'

'I should hope so too,' he said. 'She's my family. She and you.' He was standing at the window. 'Lord, here comes Gustav, and in some style! Hurry, love, we must receive them with all the formality we can manage.'

'I'll do my best.' She joined him to look down the hill at the approaching cavalcade. 'Goodness! I see what you mean about style! Regal is hardly the word! And what a throng of followers.' A cold prickle travelled down her spine. 'Are we doing the right thing, do you think? Has he outplayed us, your father?'

'I won't believe the Lissenbergers are so fickle.' He smiled at her lovingly. 'You look just right!'

She had thought a good deal about what to wear, and was pleased with the dark heavy silk that made a good background for the ceremonial necklace she now clasped around her throat with hands that shook just a little. 'I'm glad you think so.'

'For the first time, I wonder if I should have yielded to Baron Hal's persuasions and rigged myself out in knee breeches.' He glanced ruefully at his own informal dress. 'Flying in the face of everything I stand for. What do you think love?'

'I don't know,' she said. 'I just don't know. It's too late, anyway.'

'Easier for a woman.' He took her arm. 'I begin to understand why Napoleon put his court into full dress. A touch of pomp and circumstance might help at this point.'

'Ridiculous,' she said. 'Think of last year. How they shouted you into power.'

'That was last year. Ah, Baron Hals. Is it time to form the reception committee?'

'Yes, sir. And madam.' He looked anxious, suddenly old. 'The prince has brought more people than we expected, sir.'

'I noticed that. You will see that they are suitably housed.'

'In the palace, highness?'

'What do you think?' he asked Martha.

'Better here, under our eye. And maybe double the guard?'

'I don't like it,' said Franz.

'No more do I.' Smiling at him. 'But that's hardly the point, is it?'

Assiduously shepherded by Baron Hals, they joined the little group already assembled in the great hall of the palace, part of the original Gothic castle on which Prince Gustav had embroidered his baroque flourishes. Despite the enormous gilded stoves in the corners of the room, the air here struck chill as always, and Martha shivered a little as she took her place beside her husband in the centre of the little group formally arranged on the dais.

A fanfare of trumpets outside. 'He does come in style,' said Franz. 'He's even brought his own music.'

'I wonder what he has found out about Max. If anything.' They had decided that Max should be in the palace, ready to make his appearance when the moment seemed ripe.

'Nothing, I hope. Here they come.' He stiffened beside her as the big doors swung open on the last notes of the trumpets and Prince Gustav strode into the hall, the Countess of Bemberg – Princess Gertrude – at his side.

'Well,' breathed Martha. If it was not actually cloth of gold that the new princess was wearing, it certainly looked like it. 'What on earth will she wear for the performance tomorrow?' But Franz was taking the one statutory step forward to greet their guests, and she moved automatically beside him, aware of the new princess's critical eye sweeping her own dark, restrained elegance.

The first formal greetings over: 'But where is the little boy?' asked Martha.

'Such a disappointment.' Princess Gertrude had hardly spoken so far, now burst into eloquence. 'The poor baby! Not a bit well this morning. A touch of the croup. Of course I can hardly expect you to understand a mother's anxieties, highness, but I could not possibly think of bringing him out in this chilly autumn weather. My lord and master was quite angry with me, I can tell you, but, no, I said to him, home is the only place for a sick child, and I know Princess Martha will understand a mother's solicitude for her ewe lamb.'

'And the girls?' said Martha. 'You thought they should stay at home to keep their little brother company?'

'A woman's place is at home.' Prince Gustav had been carrying out a lingering survey of the great hall, as if to see what changes his successor had made. 'Or at her husband's side, of course.' His bland smile was impartially for both Martha and his wife. Then it travelled among the formally clad group waiting to greet him. 'I am glad to see that I am not the only old fogey in full dress. But where is our truant? Where is my son Max? We have a scolding for him, my wife and I, but this is hardly the time or place.'

'No,' agreed Franz, his teeth gritted. 'We have things to discuss, sir, you and I.'

'And the sooner the better. Shall we adjourn to my – I beg your pardon, dear boy, to your study?' He swept the little group with an overlord's glance. 'I can't tell you how good it is, my friends, to see so many familiar faces, but I am sure you will understand that my son and I have serious matters to discuss. And the ladies, of course, will have all kinds of things to settle about the celebration tomorrow. Just a family kind of affair I believe you have planned, but even family affairs must be conducted with a little decorum, a little ceremony. I am sure you will find Princess Gertrude an immense help to you, dear child.' It was the first time he had addressed Martha directly.

He's too clever for us, she thought angrily, as she found herself somehow involved with Princess Gertrude while the two men moved away towards Franz's study. Had she been a fool to take it for granted that she would share in their discussions? No time to think about it now, with Princess Gertrude claiming her attention, woman to woman. There was nothing she could do, short of impossibly bad manners, but see her civilly to her rooms. But deep down, she was furious with herself for not foreseeing this, and with Franz for letting it happen. And, below that still, she knew that she was very much afraid.

But Franz, when they met at last in the privacy of their bedroom, was both exhausted and triumphant. 'I really think it is going to work,' he told her. 'Oh – he's admitting nothing. He greeted Max as calm as you please, scolded him for rudely running home from his new stepmother's house. Hals was there. As he has never heard what really happened, he naturally accepted Gustav's version. It will be all over the palace tomorrow.'

'He's too clever for us,' she said it now.

'Too clever for me, you mean?' Ruefully. 'I'm sorry, my darling, I meant you to be there when we talked, but what could I do?'

'Apparently, nothing. I'm glad that at least Max was.'

'Oh, yes, but do you know, I am afraid he is still a little in awe of our father.'

'Not surprising, really.' Dryly. 'Considering how he has outmanoeuvred you both.'

'But that's the whole point,' he said eagerly. 'That's what I am trying to tell you.'

'If I would only listen?'

'Well, yes. He's agreed to everything. He is very happy as a private man, he says, but feels a duty to Lissenberg . . . He said a few hard things to me, my dear, about mistakes I have made here. I don't rightly understand our Lissenbergers, he thinks, and need his help, his advice, specially in these dangerous times with Napoleon on the rampage across Europe. And, you see, he is right about that; he had the alliance with Prussia on the line when I was only beginning to think about it.'

'I didn't see Playfair in their train.'

'No. The prince says he thinks they are not to be trusted, those two.'

'What a discovery!'

'You're angry!' He realised it at last. 'I'm sorry, love. I know you must feel left out of things. But we do have to face the facts about the Lissenbergers.'

'You mean, "A woman's place is in the home".'

'I am so glad you see it!' He had entirely missed the irony in her tone. 'It's not that I value your opinion a whit the less, it's just that I must not be seen to consult you in public. It won't do, my father says, and we have to see that he is right.'

'You called him your father.'

'Why, so I did.' They looked at each other for a long moment. 'But what I am trying to tell you is that he has agreed to everything. Little Gustav to be heir for the time being; he and Gertrude to have their own apartments in the east wing. I did her less than justice about that; she refuses to part entirely with the child, but you are to have overall supervision of his upbringing.'

'With his mother looking on.'

'She is his mother.'

'Fortunate woman.' Suddenly, Martha was too angry almost to speak. Her hands shook as she pulled off the ceremonial necklace. 'I noticed your father, as you now call him, looking round the palace with a proprietorial eye, today. Noting the improvements we have made; the comforts we have introduced. His wife, Princess Gertrude, congratulated me on making the place almost fit to live in. She was delighted with what she called the new fangled water closets in the east wing. She managed to make it sound as if she thought I was a plumber's daughter, who had been seeing to the castle's conveniences. Well, it's true. And I don't believe you have even noticed. You certainly never mentioned it.'

'I'm sorry.' Stiffly. 'Yes, I did notice. You did it while I was away. But, love, it's only money.'

'Only money! Well, what did you marry me for?' She stopped; hand to mouth; they looked at each other for a long moment, appalled.

'You know that's not true.'

'Do I?'

'Oh, my darling, what can I say?'

'Nothing.' She did not mean it for a challenge, but saw him take it as one.

10

Waking reluctant and gritty-eyed next morning, Martha wished she had had the strength of mind to banish Franz to the dressing-room, or to sleep there herself. Impossible to do so after that brief, horrifying scene, but it had meant a disastrous night. And their mutual state of jangled frustration was all wrong for this important day. He stirred a little beside her and she knew he was awake, fighting off morning. 'I'm sorry, love.' She bent down to kiss him lightly.

'You're sorry! Oh, my darling, what can I say?'

'Nothing. No need.' This time she said it lovingly. 'Let's just get through this day. Tomorrow has to be better. And, Franz – '

'Yes?'

'Forgive me for what I said?'

'No need to ask. We were both on edge, and no wonder. And anyway it's I who should be on my knees to you.'

'What an idea!' She laughed and kissed him again. 'Besides, I hear Anna with our breakfast. How I wish it was tomorrow's!'

Down at the hostel, Desmond Fylde was grumbling over an early summons from Franzosi. 'Something about the way he wants me made up,' he told Cristabel over the breakfast to which he had somewhat belatedly returned, presumably from the arms of the seconda donna. 'Tedious fellow, why could he not think of it sooner? Shall I tell him we are leaving while I am at it, my queen? I'm tired of being at the beck and call of a second-rater like him. Besides, there is something going on in town. The sooner you and I are safely out of here, the happier I shall be.'

'What do you mean?'

'Wish I knew! Something. Winks and whispers. Dry up

100

tight when they see me coming. And Prince Gustav back at the palace, behaving like the lord of creation, they say. Princess Gertrude (as we must now call that tavern keeper's daughter) is very kindly telling your friend Martha how to go on. And the palace full to bursting with Gustav's servants. I don't a bit like the sound of it.'

'No.' She thought about it. 'You are sure of this?' After she spoke, she remembered the rumours about the seconda donna and Baron Hals.

'I make a point of being well informed. And I can tell you, just as soon as you have scored your triumph tonight, and put paid to the talk about your voice, my angel, we are going to give Franzosi our notice and have some time for ourselves. I cannot do without you any longer, my own. I hope you give me credit for my strength of mind, these last days, but tonight we shall celebrate. I will make up to you for all your sad solitary nights. What a good little trouper you have been to bear it all so patiently.' He pushed down the sleeve of her négligée and planted an owner's kiss on her shoulder. 'Until tonight, my lovely. I must go while I still have the self command.'

Left alone, she amazed herself by bursting into tears.

'Curious how isolated one feels in this palace.' Count Tafur joined Martha in the great hall, where the party was grouping itself for the carriage drive down to the opera house.

'You feel it too?' She looked exhausted, he thought, and plain, despite the diamonds, the *grande tenue* of some heavy wine coloured fabric he would be hard put to describe for Lucia Aldini when he got home. 'I've been thinking,' she went on. 'I even suggested it to Franz just the other day – that when this is all over, and things are settled, I'd like to move to a house in Lissenberg itself. Just a nice, ordinary house. With no tunnels!' They were both surprised at how passionately this came out.

'What would you do with the palace?'

'It would make a wonderful hospital.'

'What a woman you are.' He looked at her with great affection. 'Funded by you, I take it?'

'Oh, money!' She flushed, then turned alarmingly pale. 'Why can one never get away from it?'

'I'm sorry – ' But he had to turn to greet Princess Gertrude, who swooped down on them, both hands outstretched, to tell Martha how well she looked.

'You make me feel dreadfully overdressed,' she concluded. 'But my lord and master would have it so. "Cloth of gold or nothing," he said, and I do know enough always to do what he tells me.' This with a quick, sharp glance for Martha.

'So you should,' said Tafur. 'Seeing what he has done for you.'

She gave him a look of overt dislike. 'Nothing is too good for the mother of his heir.' And, to Martha. 'You can have no idea, my dear, what a man feels when his son is born.'

'No, I can't, can I?' Martha gave it back to her straight. 'But I see my husband beckoning. I think it must be time to start.'

Inevitably, she shared a carriage with Prince Gustav and Max, while Franz reluctantly drove ahead with Princess Gertrude.

'I've a scold for you, daughter,' Prince Gustav had helped Martha ceremoniously into the second best state carriage. 'What have you done to my poor boy to make him look so hag-ridden today? He was happy as a grig when we parted yesterday, and now look at him! You must learn, my dear child, how to manage that husband of yours a little better. We Europeans are not perhaps quite so easy to deal with as you newcome Americans, but an intelligent young woman like you must surely be able to see this. Max and I were saying just now what a pity it is that poor Franz looks so wretched on this, which should be his – and your – great day.'

'Nothing of the kind,' said Max angrily. 'You were saying it to me, if you remember. I had not agreed. But then you do find forgetting remarkably easy, do you not? To listen to you now no one would guess what plans you had for me the other day.'

'Plans, dear boy? What plans?'

'What news do you have of little Gustav?' Martha intervened hastily to avert an explosion from Max.

'News!' Surprised. 'Oh, his illness you mean. My dear child, we are modern parents my wife and I. We see to it that our children are well looked after so that anxiety about them need not distract us from more important matters. It's – forgive me – just a trifle bourgeois to be thinking always of one's family.'

'And no one could accuse the Countess Bemberg of being bourgeois,' said Max.

'The Princess Gertrude, you mean, my boy?'

Martha was relieved to see the opera buildings ahead. 'We're almost there,' she said. 'I do hope Franzosi's opera is going to be a success.'

'I am sure he is going to surprise us all,' said Prince Gustav.

'And what precisely did he mean by that?' Max contrived to ask Martha in the little confusion of arrival.

'I wish I knew.' She had still not got used to sitting in state beside Franz in the two gilded chairs centrally and conspicuously placed to command every perspective of the ornate scenery. Nor had Prince Gustav prepared himself for his changed position in the house, which he had not attended since his fall from power the year before. There was actually a moment when Martha thought he was going to hand his wife into the left hand chair – it was almost a throne – and seat himself beside her. But Gertrude said something under her breath and he moved gracefully on to seat her in one of the chairs just below and to the side of the central ones. Martha was glad to see that Max was on the other side, below her own throne, so there was no chance of more friction between him and his father.

The audience was restless. The Lissenbergers had always been fairly respectful listeners, and in fact the little opera house did not lend itself to the kind of socialising that went on during performances in Italy, but since Franz had been in power, an opera composer himself, it had become the accepted thing that when the music started, nobody spoke. Today, no one was actually talking as the overture began, but there was a kind of rustle in the house, an expectation?

The curtain rose to reveal the Prince of Ephesus, holding court. He was passing judgment on Aegeon, a merchant of Syracuse and therefore an enemy of the state of Ephesus. There was a sigh of disappointment from the audience. These

103

were both minor characters, but were listened to in silence as they laid down the lines of the story in what Martha thought too much recitative. Aegeon was looking for his wife and their twin sons, lost eighteen years ago in a storm at sea. The prince, pitying Aegeon, gave him a day to try to find someone to pay the fine that would save his life. 'Hopeless and helpless,' sang Aegeon, knowing himself friendless in the city, and the curtain fell.

There was a sigh of anticipation from the audience as it rose again to reveal a street scene, with an ornate balcony above, and Desmond Fylde, who played both the twins, both named Antipholus, for some reason best understood by Shakespeare, with the baritone who played both Dromios, their twin servants. A fine basic comic situation, thought Martha, but why had the audience drawn a breath of such extreme pleasure?

She looked at Fylde again and saw what she had missed before, the likeness to her husband and Max. How had it been achieved? By very clever make-up, of course. The heavy eyebrows the brothers shared, and just a touch of the slav about the high cheekbones. I should have expected this, she thought, once I knew it was about twins. I'm a fool, a total, complete abject idiot. But what to do? And what use was going to be made of the likeness? A quick glance to Franz beside her told her he had not noticed it yet. One does not easily recognise oneself. Besides, she knew that he had not read the Shakespeare play. She had, but long ago. Idiotic, lunatic not to have made sure of getting hold of a copy to reread it.

Dromio left the stage to return as his twin, and to the inevitable comic misunderstanding with Fylde as the man who thought himself his master. The baritone who played both Dromios was throwing his heart into the comedy, but for the first time ever Martha actually found herself feeling sorry for Desmond Fylde. He was singing Antipholus as if it were some great serious part, Idomeneo or Aeneas. And as the opera went on she recognised that the rest of the cast were playing up to this. The whole production had been skilfully shaped around Fylde's incapacity as a comic figure. The result was to isolate him, set him up as a butt.

Was Cristabel aware of this? She thought not, since she was not involved in the knockabout element of the comedy. But she was singing superbly, surely with a new depth.

Sitting between Franz and Max, Martha was not sure which one of them first noticed Fylde's make-up, but by the end of the first act she was aware of furious tension in both of them. 'Someone's idea of a joke?' Franz leaned down to ask Max quietly as the curtain fell and the audience broke into slightly hysterical applause.

'Not one I find particularly amusing,' said Max. 'Franzosi must have tired of his position here, I think.'

'If it's only that.' But Franz had to turn away to speak to Princess Gertrude, and the curtain rose again almost at once.

The opera was in three acts. By the end of the second one, the audience was laughing every time Fylde appeared, and he was beginning to show signs of unease. Only Cristabel still seemed unaware of anything unusual, wrapped up in her own singing. She's not singing for Fylde at all, Martha realised. Can there be someone else?

The curtain fell to end Act Two. 'So,' said Franz to Max and Martha. 'What do we do?'

'Nothing,' said Max.

'I blame myself,' said Martha.

'Absurd,' said Franz.

'Dear boys,' Prince Gustav leaned across his wife. 'I do hope you are seeing the jest of this.'

'The audience is,' said Franz.

In her dressing-room, Cristabel stared into the glass as her dresser tidied her ringlets. 'Something's going on,' she said. 'What is it? They're laughing too much.'

'You haven't seen?' The dresser was amused too. 'I don't think Herr Fylde has either.'

'Seen what?'

'It's the new make-up. From the front of the house he looks just like the two princes.'

'What?' She took it all in. She had noticed, without much caring, what Franzosi was letting happen to her husband, but this was something else again. Something dangerous.

105

'Who's that?' A knock on the door. 'You know I'm never disturbed.'

But it was Doctor Joseph. 'You've seen what's going on?' he asked as their eyes met and held.

'I've only just realised. It's monstrous! What's to be done?' She turned to him with total confidence.

'Only you can do it. Turn the tables. Turn the last act into the opera seria Fylde's been singing all along. You're singing so well! I don't need to congratulate you.' They were both aware of the dresser standing by. 'Now, imagine you are Gluck's Alceste or Purcell's Dido. You have lost your husband in some great drama, not in a petty street comedy; now you find him again. You can do it.'

'Of course I can.' They both knew she would sing it for him.

By the beginning of the last act, stage confusion had confounded itself. Antipholus of Syracuse had fallen in love with Adriana's sister, played by the seconda donna, and the two Dromios were similarly embroiled. The audience was laughing harder than ever and Franzosi was having difficulty keeping his orchestra together. Fylde was badly rattled, and Martha thought that the same was true of Franz and Max. Intolerable to be made so subtly and so publicly to look fools.

A particularly vigorous bit of slapstick between Dromio and Antipholus of Syracuse brought him under the balcony where Adriana stood watching for her husband, the other Antipholus. As he left the stage, Dromio tripped Antipholus, who fell sprawling, to a roar of laughter. Impossible that this should have been rehearsed; Fylde would never have agreed to it. The way he picked himself up, obviously furious, amply proved this and sent the audience into an orgy of hoots, shouts, catcalls. In the pit, Franzosi stood pitifully irresolute, arms upraised, baton motionless.

Martha clutched Franz's hand. In a moment, the house would erupt into violence. Franzosi was obviously unable to control it. She felt Franz make to rise, but there was no way from house to stage. Hopeless. Disastrous. Then Cristabel took one step forward on the tiny upstage balcony, raised a hand with absolute authority. Martha had never seen her

106

quell a house before, but Max remembered the girl who had played Orpheus all those years ago. Amazingly, the house slowly hushed, and Cristabel began to sing. 'Where have you been, my darling, this long day?' They were restless at first, an isolated titter breaking out here and there, instantly suppressed as the music had its way with them. Martha felt a sheen of tears behind her own eyes, and reached out a hand to find Franz's, seeking hers. There was a moment when Franzosi seemed to hesitate and only the violins followed as Cristabel repeated her first line, 'Where have you been . . . ?' But Franzosi and the rest of the orchestra recognised the extra repeat for the bold act it was and came in again strongly on the next line. The audience, spellbound now, hardly seemed to notice.

From then on, they were watching grand opera. Did the rest of the cast instinctively play down the comedy, or was there less anyway in this last act? At all events, as revelation and reunion followed on each other the entire cast were singing as if possessed, the audience with them every inch of the way, while Desmond Fylde caught fire from his wife's performance and sang his own final aria with a new intensity. Only, when he folded Cristabel in his arms at last, passionately, Martha saw her head turn a little away from his, and felt a shiver of anxiety. She forgot it again as the last notes of the finale were almost drowned in a roar of applause, and the audience rose to its feet, howling for Cristabel.

The ovation went on and on, but at last Franzosi appeared, leading Cristabel on stage for a final bow. He turned, bowed low to her, then back to the audience and raised a hand for silence. What now? A public thank you for Cristabel? He looked nervous enough for anything, Martha thought, and no wonder. The audience settled gradually back into its seats, with exclamations, mutters of 'silence for the maestro', a few last calls for Cristabel. Gradually the calls for silence predominated, they came from all corners of the house, surely a pre-arranged claque.

Cristabel was still on stage. She looked at Franzosi, surprised, then paused, turned to listen, her attention helping to quiet the audience.

'Citizens of Lissenberg,' Franzosi began. 'I have been asked to speak to you tonight on a very serious subject. You will look on me, I beg, merely as a mouthpiece, a voice speaking for Lissenberg, speaking for you all. We are here, all together, celebrating the great things that happened in this very house, a year ago. Since the citizens of Lissenberg have no other chance for public discussion, I have been asked to suggest that we seize upon this one, when we are all here together, to discuss the future of the country. We all know what storm clouds are gathering around us. We have seen the messengers arriving at the palace. What have they been saying? Last year, if you remember, our new prince told us great things of democracy, of self-government for Lissenberg. I say to you, friends, that it is time we challenged him on this, asked him just what his plans are for Lissenberg, now he has finally returned from his long attendance on the great enemy, Napoleon. But, first, since this is bound to be a long and serious discussion, I suggest, my friends, that we let the ladies among the audience go home to their beds.'

Diabolically clever, thought Martha angrily. Fatally so, if the opera had ended in the expected débâcle. Monstrous to suggest that it was Franz who had betrayed his own democratic principles, when in fact it was the Lissenbergers themselves who had turned down the idea of an elected parliament. And as for the suggestion about women . . . She was aware of Princess Gertrude making as if to rise, to lead a mass evacuation of the ladies, when Cristabel took a step forward and spoke. 'My friends,' she said. 'I am not a citizen of your delightful country, but then neither, I believe, is Signor Franzosi, so it seems to me that I have quite as much right to speak to you as he has, maybe more, since I speak for myself, and he has not thought fit to mention who asked him to speak to you tonight. On all your behalf, I do so now. Signor Franzosi?'

It floored him. He had quite evidently had no instructions about this, since the assumption had been that after the disastrous end of the performance his suggestion would be carried by acclaim. He stood there for a moment, silent, his eyes on the front of the house, where the three princes sat, waiting for a cue.

It came. Prince Gustav rose to his feet. 'I did,' he said into the silence. 'I who have cared for Lissenberg for twenty-six years and have grown increasingly anxious this last year about our future. What a happy surprise it was, a year ago, what a glorious beginning, my friends! Were we, perhaps, too hopeful, carried away by the excitement of that amazing occasion? I think perhaps we were. Ah, thank you!' Two stage hands had appeared with the gilt steps that gave access to the stage.

Franz and Max were on their feet too as the audience broke into a variety of cries, the claque calling for 'Prince Gustav' while others just shouted, 'The prince' or 'All the princes'. Martha exchanged a long, questioning glance with her husband and stayed where she was as the three men climbed on to the stage, Prince Gustav inevitably in the lead. Franzosi had seized the chance to disappear, but Cristabel was still standing, very still, very quiet, at the side of the stage, watching.

Princess Gertrude leaned across to Martha. 'We should go,' she said. 'We should give the lead. This is men's work.'

'No.' She was aware that the same exchange was going on between men and women throughout the audience, and found herself wondering for a distracted second where Frau Schmidt was sitting. Because of this she missed an altercation that took place between the three men on the stage. When she looked back, she saw that Franz must have won it, and was glad. He stepped forward, and the audience hushed.

'Men and women of Lissenberg.' His trained voice had a resonance his father's had lacked. 'Prince Gustav has seen fit to call in question my fitness to rule among you, and, I rather think, my wife's. We have all seen the brilliant performance tonight – ' he turned, with a bow, to Cristabel. 'And all seen, also, a deliberate attempt to make fools of my brother and me. Oh, entertaining enough in its place, and you all know me for an enemy of censorship, but in the context of an attack on my rule, not, perhaps, very pretty. And since Prince Gustav has claimed credit for Herr Franzosi's speech, I think Prince Max and I have to thank him also for this. That is not all he has done. He has tried to kidnap me, held my brother hostage at the risk of his life. I had hoped not to have to tell you this; it is a shameful thing to have to say about one's own father. We had hoped, my wife and I, that by undertaking the upbringing of the little Prince Gustav and thus ensuring the succession for the time being, we could put an end to this unhappy dissension. We were wrong. I think, now, that I have to ask your agreement that Prince Gustav be sent into exile. Only thus, it seems to me, can we ensure peace and quiet here in Lissenberg. Have I your vote on this?'

It came in a roar, but he insisted, just the same, on a show of hands and got such an instant forest of them in favour that no one dared show against. 'Thank you,' he said at last. 'And now, my friends, since we are all here together, I think we should discuss the international threat of which Herr Franzosi spoke. It is very real. Of course we must hope that Lissenberg will be able to sit it out as neutral and I have been trying hard to ensure this, but I cannot tell you that it will be easy. There are bad times coming, and I can only promise you that we will fight our way through, or suffer them together. We have been thinking, my wife and I, how much happier we would be living in Lissenberg, among our friends, and I can tell you – and her – tonight that work has just started to convert the old town hall for our use. Martha – ' Looking down from the brilliantly lighted stage into the auditorium – 'Come and tell me you are pleased.'

She was aware of Princess Gertrude, rigid with fury, as she passed her, then friendly hands helped her up the gilt steps and she was on stage beside him, listening to the roar of the crowd. And, oddly, as she stood at his side, savouring his triumph, curtsying as he bowed, a part of her mind was with Max and Cristabel, standing together now at the side of the stage, and she knew, in her heart, that though they looked together, they were entirely apart. It was not for Max that Cristabel had sung that night.

Coming off stage at last as the excited audience began to leave, Cristabel found her husband waiting for her, his controversial make-up already removed. 'Let me be the first to congratulate you, my queen! You were tremendous! We showed them what opera should be, you and I, and so I shall tell Franzosi in the morning.'

'I doubt he'll be here in the morning to be told.' Had she really hoped to find Doctor Joseph backstage waiting to congratulate her? Waiting to solve her next problem for her, the problem of Desmond? 'At least everyone could see you had no idea of what was going on,' she told him wearily. 'I'm tired, Desmond.' She was exhausted now, the long strain of the evening catching up on her. 'God knows what is going to happen tomorrow.' How could she contrive to suggest he spend this night, like the previous ones, with the seconda donna?

'You've a right to be tired, my own. After such a performance! We'll have you home in no time, snug in your bed. And tomorrow, my life, is all our own.'

'I doubt that. The prince is bound to dismiss Franzosi and then what is going to happen to us all?' If only she was a man, she thought, she would volunteer to take over the direction of the company. 'Do you know, Desmond,' she said now. 'I think you should join the rest of the company for their after-the-performance celebration. I'm too tired, but you could find out what they are thinking.'

'Oh, no, my queen,' he told her. 'We have better plans than that, you and I. Who cares about the company? Tomorrow we will make our arrangements for Vienna. Tonight, I am all yours.'

11

'I wish I was sure exile was the answer,' Max returned to the problem next evening. 'We have to face it, he's a dangerous man, our father. It was a devilish clever plot, you know. If Cristabel had not turned the tide, that opera would have ended in a shambles, with you and me laughing stocks, and Gustav in control.'

'I know,' Franz agreed soberly. 'We owe her a great debt.'

'She says it was Doctor Joseph who suggested it,' Martha told them. 'He came to her dressing-room in the last interval. She would never have thought of it herself, she says. That's a clever man! I do hope that now you are safe away from the Trappists, Max, he will agree to come to the palace as our doctor. Or to the town hall in Lissenberg, when we move there. Now that was a surprise!' With a loving smile for her husband. 'How glad I shall be to get away from those tunnels. Personally, I would be happy to have you shut Prince Gustav up in one of the damp cells down there, rather than the honourable confinement he is in now, but I can see it is hardly the way for a son to treat his father. Even such a father. But I am afraid I do agree with Max that exile seems a dangerous alternative. He is bound to stir up trouble for us somewhere. You don't think really close confinement at Gustavsberg would be better?'

'Not now, after last night's unanimous vote for exile,' said Franz. 'I am afraid you may be right, but I think I must stand by it now. But we'll keep the little prince here as a hostage, though God knows how much that will be worth.'

'Nothing to Prince Gustav, I'd think,' said Martha. 'Maybe something to his wife. And what are you going to do about Franzosi?'

'I've done it. He has his notice to get out before the

road is closed. And Max has agreed to take his place, I'm happy to say. We are going to need all the cheerful entertainment we can get in the anxious winter I see ahead. Do you think the company is capable of putting on your opera, Max?'

'*Daughter of Odin?* I don't see why not. Cristabel would be superb as my valkyrie, but it's a long part.'

'She's a very quick study,' said Martha. 'But what about Fylde? Cristabel came to see me this morning. He wants to leave! He didn't much like what Franzosi did to him last night, and you can't really blame him.' She did not mention the other thing Cristabel had told her, that Fylde had anticipated trouble in Lissenberg. They had taken care of that, after all.

'But what of Cristabel?' asked Max. 'Does she want to go?'

'No. That's why she came to me. She can't shift Fylde, asks our help.'

'Good of her to want to stay,' said Franz. 'When the word gets out of this last performance, the world will really be at her feet. But we need her here! No use pretending it's going to be an easy winter.'

'She's a good friend,' said Martha. 'She'll stay.' Was it only that? She wished she knew, and she also hoped that Max was not reading too much into Cristabel's decision.

'Will Fylde go without her?' Max asked now.

'I doubt it. Poor Cristabel, by her very success she has tied herself more firmly to him than ever. He will never let go of such a promising source of income. And now there is her father's allowance too. No, he'll stay, I am afraid. Will that present insuperable problems for *Daughter of Odin?*'

'I don't just see him as Odin,' said Max ruefully. 'But it will be an interesting challenge to try what we can manage with the company we have, since there is hardly time to find new singers before the road is closed. I've called a special meeting of the whole company for tonight, to discuss what we are going to do. It will do them good to talk over what Franzosi tried to do, I think.'

'I'm sure it will,' said Franz. 'I'm a great believer in discussion.'

'Unlike your father,' said Martha. 'How lucky we are. And no more performances of *Night of Errors!*' To Max, but with a smile for both of them.

It had been a night Cristabel never wanted to remember, but found it impossible to forget. Satisfied at last, Desmond had fallen into a deep sleep and she managed to leave him there and make what felt like her escape to the palace and Martha's comforting company. Had she also hoped to meet Doctor Joseph there? If so, she was disappointed, but the promise of Martha's support was something.

Returning as late as possible to the hostel, she was relieved to learn that Fylde had gone down into Lissenberg. To apologise to the seconda donna for failing her the night before? He was capable of anything, she began to think. She encountered him for the first time at the meeting of the whole company with Prince Max later in the evening, and saw his start of surprise when she gave Max her promise to stay for the winter. 'I look forward to singing your valkyrie, Max.'

When the meeting ended, she made an excuse to go to her dressing-room and, as she expected, Desmond joined her there. He was very angry, she noticed wearily, but this too was only what she had expected.

'You agreed to stay!' He burst right out with it. 'Without consulting me! Your husband. Though you knew how much I want to go. You went off up to the palace and gave all kinds of promises to your friend the upstart Princess Martha, who wouldn't be a princess at all, today, if it had not been for you. And all without even mentioning it to the person most concerned. To me – your husband!'

'We have to talk about that, you and I.'

'But not tonight! How right you are, my angel. You are exhausted. I, who know and love you, can see that. Tomorrow will be time enough to talk about our careers, our future. Your great success. For tonight, it is time to go home, time for your bed, my beauty. I have thought about you all day! Thought about last night. You are the only woman for me, my angel. Never for an instant doubt that. We have sacrificed ourselves long enough. And we are never going to let any interfering old sawbones come between us again! I can't do without

114

you, my own. I've learned that.' He put a hungry hand on her shoulder.

'No.' Very quiet, very firm. 'I said we had to talk, you and I. That's why I waited here. My dresser is outside, with a couple of friends in case they are needed. I hope they won't be. Only, you must understand, there is going to be no repetition of last night.'

'Last night?' He was genuinely puzzled. 'We were happy last night.'

'You may have been. I was not. And you did not even notice. That sums it up. No need to say more. You say I'm a success. Good. If you want your share of that success, you must undertake to leave me alone. No, wait a minute.' She raised an imperious hand to silence him. 'Let me finish. I married you. I was a fool, but I married you. So – I'll work with you; I'll share my earnings with you; but from now on I will not share a bed with you. Nor a room. Understand that, respect that, and I'll let things go on, apparently, as before. Refuse – ' She paused.

'Yes, my queen, what would you do if I were to refuse? Man and wife are one flesh, remember. And woman the weaker vessel. The law is on my side.'

'The law! Here in Lissenberg, among my friends?' She looked him up and down. 'Now, are you going to your mistress, the seconda donna, or must I ask my friends to get rid of you for me?'

'Oh, I'm going where I'm wanted.' He gave in angrily. 'But I promise you, you'll be sorry!'

'I think we shall do very well.' Max was telling Martha and Franz about the meeting of the opera company over a late breakfast next morning. 'Fylde looked black as thunder, but I have Cristabel's promise, which is the main thing. She says she looks forward to singing my valkyrie. I can't tell you how grateful I am to you, Franz, for giving me this second chance, after my failure in Vienna.'

'I'm sure that was a matter of politics,' Franz told him. 'I very much look forward to seeing your opera. That's settled then.' With relief. 'What a pleasure to turn to such an agreeable subject after the chaos and confusion of the last two days! If only my friends weren't so intent on naming and taking revenge on the people they regard as my enemies, my life would be much simpler. Of course there was a claque shouting for Gustav the other night. They were paid for it. Nothing would induce me to "make examples of them" as Hals urges.'

'Here comes Baron Hals,' warned Martha.

'And in one of his panics by the look of it,' said Max. Martha's heart stirred as she saw her husband brace himself for more bad news.

'Sir! Madam!' Hals was actually stuttering a little. 'I can hardly believe it still, but the man's in the uniform of the Emperor's own guard.'

'What man?' asked Franz patiently. 'Calm yourself, baron, and tell us what guard and which emperor.'

'Forgive me. It's the shock! I'm an old man. I'm sorry.' He accepted the glass of wine Martha had silently poured and passed to him. 'Thank you.' He took a sip, hardly aware what he did. 'Sir,' to Franz. 'It's the Emperor Napoleon. He is on his way here; will arrive in half an hour; sends to warn you of his friendly visit.'

'Friendly?' questioned Franz. 'He's moved fast! What can this mean?'

'Nothing good,' said Max.

'We'd best arrange to receive him,' said Martha. 'What retinue does he bring?'

'That's what I can't understand,' said Hals. 'Just a small contingent of the Old Guard. A family visit, he calls it.'

'Trusting of him,' said Franz. 'I suppose we should take it as a compliment.'

'We might as well,' said Martha. 'But I doubt that is how it will turn out.'

Half a desperate hour later they were drawn up in the familiar position on the dais of the great hall. Hals had nervously suggested that the Emperor should be received at the castle gates, but Franz had been firm about this. 'No, that is a courtesy that must be reserved for the Emperor of Austria, our overlord. Napoleon shall have his due, nothing more.' He had also refused to free Prince Gustav, another suggestion babbled

116

by Hals, who had visibly lost his nerve. Instead, Franz had ordered the guard doubled on the guest wing. 'After this visit, we may find ourselves thinking again about Gustav's future,' he said to Max and Martha. 'For the moment, it's a comfort to have him safe in custody.'

How safe is safe? wondered Martha, as she took her place beside her husband on the dais. And how very strange to find herself, plain American Martha Peabody, waiting in full dress to receive the man many Englishmen looked on as practically the Anti-Christ himself. She had met him in Paris, when Cristabel gave a concert in Talleyrand's house, and had seen nothing to shake the dislike and distrust of him she had learned in England. Since then he had made himself Emperor, publicly murdered an innocent opponent, threatened England with invasion, and was now launching a new attack across Europe. But what in the world had made him turn aside for this extraordinary visit?

Here he was, striding into the great hall at the head of his retinue, plainly dressed as usual, sweeping off his hat in a friendly bow at the sight of her, holding out a hand to Franz who had stepped forward to greet him. 'I am come to return your visit, prince, since you left me so suddenly. Not that I blame you for that; I should have known better than to keep a man so long from his new wife.' With a civil bow for Martha.

'I bring you friendly messages from Friedrich of Württemberg,' Napoleon went on, when the first formalities were over. 'He has the kindest memories of your opera company. I shall hope to hear your diva while I am with you; I remember her well from Paris. We had a fine performance of *Don Giovanni* at Ludwigsburg just the other night. It was hard to tear myself away from so friendly a reception. But we have unfinished business to attend to, prince, you and I. May we get to it at once? If I am to catch up with my army again before it sweeps down on Vienna, I must leave you tomorrow.'

'In that case,' said Franz, 'my brother and I will be at your disposal in half an hour. Baron Hals, show the Emperor to his rooms, then send a message to the opera house commanding a performance for tonight.'

'Of *Night of Errors*, sir?' Hals looked flustered out of his wits.

'I have heard something about that,' Napoleon spoke into the little silence. 'I would like to see it.'

'Of *Night of Errors*, Hals,' said Franz.

'He wants us on his side, of course.' Franz joined Martha just in time to change for the opera. 'Or, as a grand concession, we may remain neutral and send him all our mineral exports.'

'Tempting,' said Martha.

'But we refused.'

'I'm glad. What will he do now?'

'What can he do? Just because he found he could win young Friedrich of Württemberg with promises of a crown, he thinks he can carry everything before him. We'll show him different, here in Lissenberg.'

'What in the world made him think he could persuade you so easily?' It still troubled Martha. 'After trying all summer, and failing.'

'It's the problem of great power,' said Franz cheerfully. 'You end up convinced you can do anything. I'm glad I shall never be anything but the most minor of princes. Are you ready, love? We must not keep our great man waiting.'

Napoleon was in the great hall, talking to a member of the Old Guard, Baron Hals dancing anxious attendance. The soldier was exhausted, mud-stained, dishevelled. 'I couldn't stop him, sir,' Hals saw Franz and began to excuse himself. 'He insisted on seeing the Emperor at once.'

'Why not?' asked Franz. 'Our honoured guest.'

'A little more than that,' said Napoleon. 'I have news for you, prince. My troops are now in control of both Brundt and Lissenberg. No need to look alarmed – quite without bloodshed – all your friends are safe. But you must see that it means a reopening of our discussion.'

'I don't believe it,' said Franz. 'It's not possible.'

'Nothing is impossible to a mind like mine. And you were the greatest help to me, my dear prince. I promise to remember it in my arrangements for you and your charming wife. If you had not grown impatient and hurried home across the mountains, how would I have found the way?'

'You had me followed?'

'Naturally I had you followed. Carefully. A rough path, but my trained mountaineers seem to have managed it. And of course the element of surprise was complete. I am happy to be able to tell you that we have taken control quite unopposed. Look out the window, if you need proof. It is my guard on duty now, not yours. Your Lissenbergers are a sensible, peace-loving people. I believe I will not insist on their serving in my army, just so long as they keep the munitions flowing. And I have just this minute hit on the way to make sure of that. They do seem to be remarkably fond of you – and your princess – ' another of his bows for Martha – 'I think if we lock you up comfortably here in the palace and let it be known that it will be the dungeons for you if supplies falter – Don't you think, princess, that your friends will see to it that I get my weapons.'

'Blackmail,' said Franz, between his teeth.

'Power politics, my dear young friend. If you are ever to rule again, you will need to learn more about them. But for the time being, I am afraid you and your wife must resign yourselves to the most honourable form of captivity. Just so long as your Lissenbergers behave themselves.'

'And you will govern in my place?'

'I'd thought about that brother of yours – Ah, here he is – But I'm afraid that won't do, will it?' He turned to Max, who had been brought in by two of the Old Guard. 'Welcome to our discussion, prince.'

'Treachery,' said Max.

'I was just explaining to your brother. We have a phrase in France, "*A la guerre comme à la guerre.*" Would you translate that as, "All's fair in love and war"?'

'I don't see what love has to do with it.' Max was white with fury.

'Ah, but you will. You three are to be hostages for the good behaviour of your loving Lissenbergers.'

'And Prince Gustav?' asked Franz.

'A good question.' Napoleon turned as if to an approved pupil. 'I really think Prince Gustav poses a problem for all of us. And one about which I propose to consult an expert. Is Prince Joseph there?' He barked the question at one of his staff.

'He waits your pleasure, sire.'

'Then send him in.'

Brother Joseph? Doctor Joseph? Prince Joseph? He had shed his monk's habit and was elegant in court black and stark white cravat. 'I am to ask your pardon.' He kissed Martha's hand, and, surely, pressed it very slightly. In friendship, in warning? 'And yours,' to Franz and Max. He held out a hand. 'I'm glad to meet you honestly at last, brothers.'

'Brothers? Are you mad? What kind of a jest is this?' Franz turned angrily back to Napoleon.

'One at your expense, prince. As you will find. I told you that your father presented a problem. I do not think you have quite understood just how much of one. My investigators found Prince Joseph easily enough, and there is not the slightest question of the validity of his claim to Lissenberg. Prince Gustav met his mother when he was a young man on the grand tour, passing through Switzerland. She was the daughter of an aristocratic Lutheran family. There was nothing for it but marriage, so of course he married her. And equally of course abandoned her before the boy was born. Luckily for him – and for you two – she died soon afterwards. Her family gave the child their name and brought him up as their own. They never told him who his father was, not even when Gustav became Prince of Lissenberg. But there is not the slightest shadow of a doubt that he is your older brother and therefore heir to Lissenberg.'

'A bought title,' said Franz. 'I think the Lissenbergers would have something to say to that.'

'If they were asked,' said Napoleon. 'But they are not going to be, are they? They are going to be told. The only question is,' to Joseph, 'by you or by me?'

'Oh, by you, I think, sire,' said Joseph. 'It is you, after all, who have come, seen and conquered. I merely prepared the ground.'

'Treachery!' said Max again.

'I do hope that you will see in the end that it is merely

120

common sense,' Joseph addressed himself now to both his brothers. 'The Emperor is going to conquer Europe, you know. Nothing will stop him, and a very good thing for Europe it will be. You know as well as I do that it was time for a breath of modern air on these decadent principalities. Freedom of trade, freedom of thought, freedom of worship! Napoleon brings them all. You must know that in your heart.' He turned to address Franz directly. 'Since you yourself supported him with passion back in your student days in Paris. And you,' to Max, 'have surely seen enough of the antique tyranny of what used to be the Holy Roman Empire to recognise the advantage of throwing in Lissenberg's lot with the winning side, when it also happens to be that of enlightenment? And I tell you, brothers, Napoleon promises great things for Lissenberg. Our independence, and a road across the mountains, built by his engineers. All in exchange for willing co-operation.'

'Willing?' asked Franz.

'And the Duc d'Enghien?' asked Martha quietly.

'A mistake, ma'am.' Napoleon gave her a quick, sharp look. 'One that won't happen again. But it is more than time we left for the opera house. You don't want your Lissenbergers cooped up there too long with their anxiety about you. Have I your word of honour, gentlemen, that you will not try to cause trouble, or must I leave the princess behind as hostage for your good behaviour?'

Franz and Max exchanged a quick look. Then: 'You have our word.'

'Thank you. And here, in the nick of time, is our last guest.' They had all heard sounds of arrival outside. 'Greet the lady,' Napoleon told Baron Hals. 'And bring her here. My guards have orders to obey you. And while we wait for her,' to Joseph, 'tell me whether you think your father should be present for the announcement tonight?'

'No,' said Joseph. 'He has no part to play in this.'

But no one was paying attention. All eyes were fixed on the big doors which had been thrown open to admit a flamboyant, well-remembered figure. Minette de Beauharnais had grown from a pretty girl to a striking young woman. The blond curls that had tended to straggle a little had been swept up into a Grecian knot, the slightly vacuous pink and white face had

121

achieved a firm hint of character. 'Uncle, I'm late! Forgive me!' She swept up the hall, her Parisian draperies making every woman feel a frump.

'You are just in time.' He accepted her kiss with more pleasure than Martha had expected, held her affectionately in his arm as he presented Prince Joseph. 'The other princes I believe you know of old.'

'I most certainly do.' With a wicked look for Max. 'And dear Martha! What happiness to meet you again. And to congratulate you on your marriage.'

'You should congratulate me,' said Franz.

'Is it just the moment for that? But of course I do, most heartily. And I look forward to hearing my other old friend, Cristabel the other married lady, sing for us. She is quite the rage here in Lissenberg, by what I hear.' Another naughty look for Max. 'Am I to condole with you, prince?'

12

There was no chance for a private word before they reached the opera house, hardly time for thought. Minette de Beauharnais insisted on driving with Martha and Franz, and kept up a constant stream of chatter: about Paris, about parties, and above all about her Uncle Napoleon whom she seemed to adore. When they arrived, Martha had the sensation of being in a dream, helpless. Napoleon was being received with military honours by his own troops, drawn up outside the opera house. Behind them, she could see the anxious faces of the mass of Lissenbergers who had not found room within.

Inside, the house was hushed, almost deadly quiet, as Napoleon walked briskly to the one gold chair that awaited him, and the rest of them found their places below and beside him. What now? A rattle of drums, the orchestra struck up the '*Marseillaise*', and the audience shuffled awkwardly to its feet, presumably warned in advance. Martha's hand reached for her husband's. Joseph had vanished; the rest of them sat still in their places at the front of the house.

When it was over, Joseph appeared on the stage. Briefly, unemphatically, he told them what had happened, ending with Napoleon's guarantee that no one would be hurt so long as everyone co-operated, and his promise of a road out through the mountains. This got him a faint cheer, the first reaction from the stunned audience. Martha felt the tension in the house, alive, dangerous. Joseph must be aware of it too. He ended on a sombre note, half threat, half promise, stepped back: 'Let the opera begin.'

The orchestra plunged into the overture with a good deal more enthusiasm than it had showed for the '*Marseillaise*'. The audience gave a little sigh, and Martha grasped Franz's hand convulsively. No way Napoleon could know yet, but this was the overture not to *Night of Errors* but to last year's prize-winning opera, Franz's own *Crusader Prince*. Joseph would know. What would he do about it? What could he? And how would Napoleon react when it dawned on him that instead of this year's comic opera, mocking the twin princes, he was watching the one that had sparked off last year's revolution? Cristabel's idea, of course, and Franzosi, under notice, did not care what he did. They must have rehearsed like demons all afternoon. Franz's music was coming over even more powerful than Martha remembered it.

The curtain rose at last to show Desmond Fylde, the crusader prince, taking leave of his wife and court. Sitting beside and below him, Martha felt rather than saw Napoleon recognise what was happening. He did not move a muscle. Whatever he would do, he was not going to do it yet. Joseph, beyond Minette on the other side, was equally still. Desmond Fylde seemed nervous at first, and she could hardly blame him, but Cristabel was singing like someone possessed, and gradually the rest of the cast caught fire from her. This was going to be a memorable performance in more senses than one. The audience, restless and rustling with surprise to begin with, had sensed this too. It was going to be one of the rare occasions when an opera becomes more than a public performance, becomes a ritual shared by singers and audience. Martha's last detached thought, before she surrendered to the group emotion, was to wonder what in the world Cristabel would do with her last aria, the one that Franz had secretly rewritten last year, so that her final call for freedom was actually the signal for revolution. Franz must be thinking of this too. Whatever happened, they were in for it. His hand pressed hers. Whatever the outcome, this was worth it.

Desmond Fylde strode off to the wars. Cristabel appeared, ravishing as always in tunic and hose, disguised as a page to follow him, and the curtain fell for what should have been the one long interval. But the orchestra went on playing. The audience, restless for a few moments, stilled to listen as Franzosi, at the fortepiano, skilfully led his musicians through a series of variations and so into the second act overture. Nobody stirred. Risking a glance, Martha saw Napoleon sitting very still, apparently absorbed. Nothing was going to happen. Not yet.

The second half went even better than the first, she thought, and felt Franz thinking so too. He had written the part specially for Cristabel, and she was superb. Chained in a dungeon because her husband had never recognised the page who had saved his life, and had come home to accuse her of unfaithfulness, she sang only of hope and forgiveness. For a moment Martha's concentration failed; would she and Franz find themselves in a dungeon tonight? In separate dungeons?

Now Cristabel was facing the ordeal of red-hot ploughshares and emerging in triumph, unscathed. At last, she threw off her white penitent's robes, to reveal herself in page's doublet and hose and accept her husband's recognition and anguished call for pardon. She moved forward and a shiver went through the audience as she began her final aria. Last year it had been a summons to battle, this year she made it a dirge. 'Freedom,' she sang at last. 'Freedom . . . freedom,' on a dying fall.

Tears were running down Martha's cheeks. She had not cried all day, found it a relief and wondered how many women in the audience were doing the same. Last year, the opera had ended violently at this point, but now the chorus took one step forward for Franz's finale. It should have been a paean of hope for the future, a rousing chorus of love and joy, but here too something had subtly changed. The words were the same; the music the same; what they did with them was another matter, sad beyond belief. And, gradually as they sang, one after another, they moved quietly off the stage, until only Cristabel was left. She moved forward, looked straight at Napoleon on his golden throne and sang, very quietly, the words of her aria again: 'Freedom, freedom, freedom . . .' She dropped him a deep curtsy, and the curtain fell.

No revolt this time. The applause was passionate but subdued, Cristabel's message taken. And before it had ended Napoleon was on his feet, his guards clearing a passage for him, the audience backing to left and right, whispering together, and the rest of the court followed him out. A hand reached out to touch Martha's. 'God keep you,' breathed Frau Schmidt.

There was a guard in the carriage with them on the way back, and when they reached the castle he shepherded them into the great hall, where Napoleon now stood on the dais. Franz's hand was firm on hers. So long as we are not separated, she thought, I can face anything, and knew he was thinking it too.

Napoleon was formidably calm. 'I must congratulate you on your opera.' He did not give Franz his title. 'And on the common sense of the Lissenbergers. We should have all been sorry if the evening had ended differently.' It was the most restrained of icy threats. 'And I am glad to think you will have no trouble in earning a living, when I see fit to release you to do so. Next spring, maybe, when the winter's production from your mines is safe in my hands, and work on the road has begun. And I hope you will use your enforced inactivity this winter to write me an opera as good as the one we have just heard. I will not venture to suggest a theme.' He turned to Joseph. 'Close guard, I think, for both your brothers until winter shuts the road out. After that, I leave it to your discretion, as I do so much else. And now, I'll say goodbye since I must be on my way first thing in the morning. I leave everything in your capable hands, Prince Joseph.'

'You may,' said Joseph.

Formal goodnights. A nightmare of civilities. Martha wanted to scream, to curse, to break through this masquerade. Franz's hand on hers was a warning. There was nothing to be gained by a scene, much to be lost. Minette kissed her goodbye. 'Take care of yourself and your brilliant husband, my dear creature, and I shall look forward to seeing you in the spring. And you – ' This, with emphasis, for Joseph.

'At your service.' Had she intended him to kiss the hand she held out?

No chance of a word alone with Max. As Napoleon turned away, their guard was at their side, leading them, thank God, to their own apartments. Not the cold cells tonight. But there were new locks on their doors. 'I shall be outside,' said the guard, ushering them in.

The door closed behind them and they heard him lock it

126

from outside. Franz pressed her hand, let it go and moved swiftly across the room to the panel that masked the secret door to the passage and tunnel. As they had both expected, it had been fastened securely on the other side.

'My fault,' said Martha. 'I trusted Joseph.'

'Oh, fault! If we are to speak of fault! My darling, I led Napoleon's army through Lissenberg's secret way. Will I ever live that down?'

'I think you're forgiven already, don't you? That was a wonderful audience tonight, did you feel it as I did?'

'Yes, full of love. Did you notice, Joseph did not need to say anything about the threat to us? They knew already.'

'And putting on your opera was their answer. God bless Cristabel!'

'A remarkable woman. That interval music was a masterpiece, too, and I don't for a moment think it was Franzosi's idea.'

'Your opera is a masterpiece. Do you realise, Franz, that if we can survive this winter we will be free, come spring, to make our own lives where we want to? I do hope that makes you as happy as it does me.'

'My darling, I have been thinking of nothing else.' He moved over to shoot the bolt on the inside of the apartment door. 'And I have been thinking, too, that for the first time since we married, we are really alone together, you and I. No Baron Hals knocking on the door with a long face and a new crisis to be dealt with. I was only afraid of one thing today. That we would be separated.'

'Me too.' She threw grammar to the winds and walked into his eager embrace.

Down at the opera house, Cristabel sat wearily in front of her dressing table, gazing unseeingly into the glass. 'You should go home, my lady,' urged her dresser. 'Everyone else has gone. Herr Fylde went long since.' Was this intended as comfort or condolence?

'Yes, I saw.' He had gone very attentively with the seconda donna, and with one sharp glance back to her, where she had still stood receiving the eager compliments of the company. In which he had not joined. He was gone, and would not come back, and she was glad. But she had never in her life felt so alone.

Betrayed. Joseph had betrayed them all. Not Doctor. Prince, and traitor. There had not been time to face it before, since her first thought, on hearing the shocking news from the palace, was that Franz and Max must not be mocked by a repetition of *Night of Errors*. It had been a hard fight to achieve the changeover, and a harder one to make it work. Now, at last, she had the rest of her life to face how he had betrayed her. And his brothers. Doctor Joseph had been Prince Joseph all the time, spying on them, plotting against them. She would never trust anyone again. She tried not to remember the moments when she had felt her mind and body beat in time with his. Not felt, imagined. Had she really imagined a future with him at her side? Was this why she had given Fylde his notice to quit?

Her dresser was saying something. 'I'm sorry,' she said wearily. 'I'm keeping you up. You're right, it's time to go. It's all over.'

Back at the hostel, there was Lady Helen to be faced. 'You were brilliant, my dear child. Your idea of course.'

'Thank God it worked. I really think there will be no violent resistance now, so no danger to Martha and Franz.'

'And Max.'

'Yes. I wonder what Prince Joseph means to do with Lissenberg, now he has it.' Her voice hardened on the title.

'Prince Joseph indeed! No wonder he seemed to take so much upon himself. But can that story really be true?'

'I'd believe anything of Prince Gustav. It sounds just like him. And, after all, there are enough of his bastards about, here in Lissenberg. I suppose that is why one didn't notice the likeness between Joseph and his brothers. I see it now. I wish to God I'd seen it sooner.' She changed the subject abruptly. 'What shall we do, aunt? Go, or stay?'

'I've been thinking about that. I think we should go to Venice, my dear. To your mother. Count Tafur will be delighted to give us his escort.'

'And leave Martha to her fate? I don't think I can do that, aunt. Not after all she has done for me.'

'Do you think you can be a help to her?'

'I can at least try.'

Waking, very tired, totally happy, in her husband's arms, Martha lifted her head at a knocking on the door.

It had waked Franz too. He smiled up at her sleepily. 'Not Baron Hals!' he said.

But it was. Or rather it was Anna, asking in some agitation, if Martha would see the Baron without delay. 'I know it's early, but it's the lady, you see, Mademoiselle de Beauharnais, she's not well, she wants to stay.'

'I'll be with him in five minutes,' said Martha. 'What are you laughing at?' she asked Franz.

'I was thinking that I may not be needed any more, but you clearly are,' he said. 'And I was also thinking, "poor Joseph".'

'Yes.' She was dressing rapidly as they talked. 'I must say I find myself sorry for him too. That's a very determined young woman.'

'She means to be Princess of Lissenberg.' He laughed again. 'And you are to chaperone her until she has Joseph in line.'

'While you write an opera for Napoleon?' She bent to kiss him, happily aware of the new ease between them.

'Not for Napoleon.' He pulled her down to him for a long moment. 'You had better be off to your duties, my one and only love, or I shall never let you go.'

'Do you think I'll be more successful as a chaperone than I was as a princess?' She was combing her hair.

'Royalty not really our line?' He smiled at her lazily. 'For me, my love, you will always be perfect.'

Minette de Beauharnais had already established herself in the wing that had been used by Napoleon, and had arranged a fine invalid scene for Martha's benefit. She was lying on a *chaise longue*, sal volatile at the ready, her maid hovering in attendance. For a moment, Martha wondered if she was really ill; there was something hectic about the red in her cheeks.

'That will do.' She dismissed her maid, held out her arms. 'Dear Martha, it's so good to see you. Now, we are to plot together, you and I, to make this winter's confinement as tolerable as possible for us all. What do you do when the snow comes down and the roads are closed?'

Last year I was helping my husband govern Lissenberg. She did not say it. 'I am afraid you may be very much bored, Minette. Are you sure you have made a wise decision? It is not too late to follow Napoleon. Or in a few days even. The roads are not usually closed for some time yet. And just imagine if he really takes Vienna.'

'Of course he is going to take Vienna.' Pettishly. 'But Lissenberg is what he has offered me.'

'That's frank, at all events. So you have Napoleon's permission to stay?'

'I wouldn't be here otherwise! The thing was, we had neither of us seen this Joseph. He might have been entirely impossible, brought up by *petit bourgeois* Swiss, but he's twice the man his brothers are. There's no Swiss inamorata in the background, I do hope.'

'Not that I know of,' said Martha. 'But then, I know so little about him. What would Napoleon have done if he had not thought him fit to rule here?'

'God knows!' Shrugging. 'He keeps his own counsel mainly, does Uncle Napoleon. But what a man! What a conqueror! I'm glad I'm not in Vienna just now. He'll come down on them like the wind from the west. And we shall be snug here, as merry as mice in Lissenberg. But, tell me, my dear creature, about my old friend Max. Is he still wearing the willow for Lady Cristabel, despite her marriage?'

'I am afraid so.' Martha thought this a bit of information Minette had better have.

'Hopeless, of course. That's a very handsome fellow, Cristabel's tenor. I remember noticing him in *Crusader Prince* last year. Is it true that he is descended from a line of Irish princes?'

'He has often said so.'

'So, not entirely a misalliance for dear Cristabel. And, after all, she had hopelessly down-classed herself by taking up singing. You know as well as I do, love, that in Paris we look on our opera singers as little better than ladies of the streets.'

'Yes,' said Martha. 'But I do urge you to remember, Minette, that Lissenberg is not Paris.'

'No, indeed.' Sighing. 'I can see I am going to be immensely bored here. But you and I are going to do something about that, my dear. After all, you have lost your occupation. What better than for the two of us to apply our minds to arranging a little entertainment for this long winter of confinement. Talking of which, you have not thanked me for persuading Joseph to release you from your captivity.'

'I did not know that I had you to thank for it.'

'But, of course. Who else would have troubled?'

'Then I thank you. May I ask if it applies to Franz too?'

'So long as he behaves with common sense. I believe he and Max are with their brother now. Remarkable for them suddenly to have acquired an older brother, is it not?'

'The amazing thing is, I still like Joseph.' Franz was telling Martha about his meeting with Joseph and Max. 'And so does Max. He's betrayed us, spied on us, and we can't help liking him.'

'And so do I,' said Martha. 'I was thinking, myself, how odd it is. And when you say betrayed . . . I'm sure he didn't betray our meeting-place to Gustav's men that night.'

'No. Why should he? He knew all he had to do was wait for Napoleon and the Old Guard.'

'He knew they were coming?'

'Oh, yes. I am afraid we have to face it, love, Napoleon's communications are a great deal more efficient than ours have ever been, here in backward Lissenberg.'

'Why shouldn't we be backward? Myself, I like it!'

'Spoken like a true Lissenberger.' Lovingly. 'And, curiously enough, that is very much what Joseph said to Max and me.'

'How do you mean?'

'He says he's grown to love Lissenberg in the months he's been here, spying out the land. Oh, he makes no bones about that. Why should he? The story he told is quite true, you see, up to this spring when Napoleon's people found him. He lost his grandparents and his livelihood when the French moved into Switzerland; found himself in the French army, that's how they discovered him. Imagine suddenly finding himself a prince, with a solid claim even to little Lissenberg! He didn't

131

know his mother's story; just thought his parents long dead. Of course he wanted to come here, take a look at his father – not to mention his brothers.' He smiled at her. 'He says he likes us too!'

'And loves Lissenberg? So, what is he going to do?'

'No question about that. He is going to hold Lissenberg for Napoleon. In fact, granted the garrison the Emperor left, he has no choice. But there is no doubt in the world that he honestly believes both that Napoleon is going to conquer Europe and that it is a good thing he should do so. It will mean an end to customs barriers, he says, to all those small feuds and fights – Well, look at Italy!'

'I wonder if Count Tafur would agree with you.'

'Have you seen the count today?'

'Yes. He came to see me while you were with Joseph.'

'You must call him prince.'

'So I must. Your older brother! How strange it all is. Count Tafur is leaving us, and I don't blame him. He says he thinks he can do so now that Lady Helen is back. I'm afraid it means he looks on poor Cristabel's case as hopeless. Which of course it is.'

'Well, not entirely,' said Franz. 'Not after the two performances she has just given. I hope she doesn't mean to leave us, Martha.'

'She promised not to, before any of this happened. She'll keep her word, I'm sure of it.'

'If her husband lets her.'

'I'm not sure what he says will make much difference. She has changed a great deal. I don't know what's happened, but she's changed. Well, think of the way she has carried things, these last two performances.'

'Like the great lady she is. Poor Cristabel.' He smiled and took her hand. 'Do you realise, my darling, that this is quite the longest uninterrupted conversation we have had since we were married. I begin to think there is a lot to be said for not being Prince of Lissenberg.'

'But what is going to happen to you – to us? Has Prince Joseph said?' This time she gave Joseph his title without thought.

'He wants us all – you and me and Max – to stay in the

palace for the time being. Under his eyes, he says. But as advisers, too.'

'You'll run the opera house between you? You and Max?'

'Just so.'

'What about Franzosi?'

'My dismissal of him stands.' He laughed. 'I think Joseph is glad to be able to use him as scapegoat for putting on *Crusader Prince*. Lord, we might have been in trouble!'

'I felt the dungeons looming, didn't you?'

'You have to admit the Emperor behaved with great dignity.'

'Yes,' she said thoughtfully. 'I do.'

Calling on Cristabel to take his leave, Count Tafur found her and Lady Helen presiding over a great moving of furniture in the star's apartments. Since he had met Fylde's valet on the stairs with a long face and an armful of his master's clothes over his arm, he had a fairly good idea of what was going on. 'I am to congratulate you?' He kissed Cristabel's hand with his invariable old-fashioned courtesy, but thought she looked exhausted and her aunt anxious.

'You could say so.' She managed a travesty of a smile. 'Up to a point. We have agreed to live apart, my husband and I.'

Martha had been right, he thought, there was a new certainty, a new dignity about Cristabel, but something was very wrong, just the same. 'Will Fylde stay in Lissenberg?' he asked.

'Oh, I think so, since I do.' Unspoken between them was the knowledge that Fylde would stay to keep an eye on his investment. 'But my aunt is coming back to live with me. You may certainly congratulate me on that.'

'I do indeed. Both of you.' With a smile for Lady Helen. 'And I will give your comparatively good news to your mother.' What else was there to be said? He rose to go, but she put out an eager hand to detain him.

'But, please, before you go, tell us what is going on at the palace? What happened last night? Martha and Franz? Max? He's not harmed them? The upstart prince! Traitor! Hypocrite!' She spat it out.

'Far from it.' He could feel the tension in her, coiled, dangerous. 'In fact, I've just been with Martha and can't think when I've seen her so happy, so relaxed. No – no cold cells for them last night, and Franz and Max have been with their brother this morning. It's a very strange business, but I think it is too early to call that young man traitor or hypocrite.'

'What? Coming here in disguise? Napoleon's spy! Currying favour with Martha? With us all? Worming out our secrets in the guise of priest and doctor? I tell you, count, if I could have killed him last night, I'd have done so.'

'Well,' he said pacifically. 'I think you will probably live to be glad that you could not.'

When he had left, Lady Helen crossed the room to sit down by Cristabel and take her hand, a rare gesture. 'Something is wrong, my dear. Tell me what it is? What can I do to help?'

'Nothing, aunt. Everything! I wish I was dead.'

When Tafur got back to the palace he found a summons to the new prince.

'You are leaving us, I hear.' Prince Joseph was sitting at what had been his father's and then his brother's desk, surrounded with papers.

'With your permission, prince.'

'Oh, that's of course. But I hope you do not mean to take Lady Cristabel with you. We are going to need her badly here this winter. That was a brave thing she did last night. She seems to know more than any of us about these strange people, the Lissenbergers. I didn't think it would work, but I'm very glad it did.'

'And that it got a chance to,' said Tafur dryly.

'Oh, the Emperor is a great man. And he has his instincts too. But – you've been to see Lady Cristabel – will she stay?'

'Yes. She tells me she had already promised the princess that she would. What has happened only makes her more determined to do so.'

'That's good. Tell me, count – ' He was suddenly, surprisingly, human. 'Is she very angry with me?'

134

'Yes.'

'She has every right to be. I wish you would tell her . . . No, there's nothing . . . What could I say? Her husband will stay too?'

'I assume so.' Well informed as he was, Prince Joseph doubtless knew about their separation already.

'I suppose he will. Please convey my respectful greetings to the Signora Aldini, count, and my wishes that next year we may persuade her to visit us, to find, I hope, that we are not entirely barbarous here in Lissenberg. We will do everything to see that her daughter does not regret her decision to stay.'

'I am sure she will not, so long as her friend the princess is safe and happy.'

'I think I can promise that too. Prince Gustav and his train are on their way back to Gustavsberg, to a much more stringent form of captivity than they had endured previously. That dream of his is over for good.'

'And little Gustav?'

'I would not dream of separating mother and child. And it's early to be worrying about an heir in the next generation.'

'With three able bodied princes in this one.' Count Tafur found himself liking the man more and more. 'But I am taking too much of your time.' He glanced at the paper-strewn table.

'The future of Lissenberg. I studied a little engineering before I turned to medicine. It is the question of the road out through the mountains. I have been studying the ground all summer and hope that when the Emperor sends his experts, as he has promised to do before the pass is closed, we will be able to make a good start on our planning, before the deep snow. Who knows, maybe you and the Signora Aldini will be able to come to us by an easy route next year? Do give her my kind regards.' And with this reiterated message he ended the interview.

'The new road next year?' Martha was amazed. 'It would change everything.'

'It would guarantee Napoleon uninterrupted military supplies from the mines at Brundt,' said Franz.

'But if he is certain of conquering Austria in this campaign, will that be so important to him?' Max asked.

'He's a soldier,' said Franz. 'That's where I think our brother is wrong about him. Joseph thinks that presently he will be satisfied, and stop.'

'The question is where, isn't it?' Tafur had come to say goodbye to the three of them. 'Not at the Rhine, so, at the Elbe, the Oder – '

'Or the Indus,' said Martha. 'There was something Minette said, made me wonder.'

'Do you know,' Tafur was on his feet, ready to leave, 'in our long talk, Prince Joseph said not a word about her.'

'Well, poor fellow,' said Max. 'He hardly would, would he?'

'He sent the kindest messages to Lucia.' Tafur kissed Martha on the cheek. 'And has invited her to come and visit Cristabel next year.'

'Do try and persuade her,' said Martha eagerly.

'Next year,' said Franz, and a small silence fell.

13

Deferring as prettily as possible to Martha in public, Minette de Beauharnais made it crystal clear in private that she looked on herself as senior lady in the palace. 'Of course, as a princess by marriage, you must take public precedence over me, dear Martha, but we must never forget that I represent my uncle here.'

'No, indeed.' Oceans deep in her honeymoon with Franz, Martha was too happy to care.

'So,' Minette went on, satisfied, 'it is my duty to think how to smooth over any little awkwardness that remains in our situation. I think a modest entertainment, don't you, love? A party for the élite of Lissenberg, with dear Cristabel to sing for us. I understand that there might be a little difficulty to be ironed out between her and Prince Joseph, since he actually acted doctor to her.'

'He is a doctor, and a good one.'

'Made of talents! And an engineer as well, would you believe it? You should see his study, full of the most extraordinary drawings. And so much business! No time for us ladies yet, but he gave me carte blanche for my little party, referred me to you for the details. You'll be pleased to hear he insists that our dear Cristabel come as guest as well as entertainer. Oh, and there are a couple of other people he wants invited, said you'd know where to find them: a Frau Schmidt and someone called Ishmael Brodski.' Doubtfully. 'Can that be right? Will he be quite the thing?'

'It depends a little what kind of thing,' said Martha. 'But I will be delighted to invite them both. When are you proposing to give this little party?'

'Oh, soon, don't you think?'

'Yes, best before the weather gets bad, if some of the guests are coming from Brundt.'

137

'Next week then. I'm sure, admirable Hausfrau that you are, you can manage everything by then. And I shall treat myself to driving down to call on Cristabel, congratulate her on both her performances, and command her appearance. Do you think she and that handsome husband of hers would sing some of the duets from *Night of Errors*? I quite long to hear that opera! Well,' without giving Martha time to reply, 'I must be off if I am not to be benighted on my way back. I'll give your love to Cristabel, shall I?'

Left alone, Martha sighed and smiled, and started making a guest list. Franz and Max were down at the opera house busy with the inevitable reorganisation, since Franzosi had gone the day before. She, too, had been busy enough in the few days since Napoleon had left. The whole palace had been in a state of shock and confusion. Prince Gustav and his train had left their apartments in chaos. Prince Joseph had refused to move into the royal apartments she shared with Franz, saying that he preferred the Blue Rooms. The housekeeper, the groom of the chambers, the cook and even Baron Hals had come to her, one after the other, to protest, to complain, to grumble, even to threaten she did not quite know what. Or want to. She had made this crystal clear, calmed them, soothed them, and sent them back to work. Would this party be a last straw, or might it not prove a useful distraction?

She was wondering whether Ishmael Brodski would accept, and what the Lissenberg aristocracy would think if he did, when Baron Hals appeared with a summons to Prince Joseph's study. 'If it is convenient. He says he knows how busy you are.'

'Civil of him.' She rose, shook out her skirts. 'I'll come at once.'

She had not seen Prince Joseph alone since he had been Doctor Joseph and helped her smuggle Franz out of the palace. How strange it all was. He looked exhausted, visibly older now than his two brothers, his newly cropped hair emphasising the family likeness.

'No, no.' He forestalled her curtsy as Hals closed the door. 'I'm your brother, remember. And proud to be.' Kissing her firmly on both cheeks. 'And I have an immense apology for you, and a heartfelt thank you. Don't think I haven't known how you have been easing things for me, here in the palace. Without you, I don't know how I would have gone on. There is more to taking over a country than guards in the streets, and so I am beginning to learn. But, sit down, please, and tell me if you think we are going to pull through.'

'Oh, I think so, don't you? Franz says Lissenberg itself is calm enough, but there is always the problem of Brundt.'

'Yes. We still have guards on duty there, I'm sorry to say, and a curfew. If there is going to be trouble, that is where it will start.'

'And where the mines are.'

'Just so. This party Mademoiselle de Beauharnais wants, do you think it a good idea?'

'Admirable, if it works.'

'If they come, you mean. Frau Schmidt and the senior citizens of the town. And your friend Brodski, whom I badly want to meet.'

'He'll come, if I ask him. And Frau Schmidt, but the other town elders . . . I'm not sure about them.'

'The ones who backed your husband as revolutionary and found themselves landed with him as prince.'

'Just so.'

'Oh, well, they will just have to learn that now they are landed with me. But, tell me – I am going to take a brother's privilege and call you Martha – may I?'

'Of course.'

'Lady Cristabel.' He hesitated, then plunged into it. 'Will she forgive me, do you think?'

'She's very angry.' It had surprised Martha. 'She won't talk about it.'

'She has a right to be angry. But what could I do? Martha – what could I do? And I am a doctor.'

'And you did her good. But that's hardly the point.'

'I know.' She had never seen him so subdued. 'But,' more hopefully, 'that bold choice of *Crusader Prince*! Her doing, of course. She took a great risk.'

'Not for you.' Martha felt it must be said.

'No, for my brothers, of course, and for you.'

'And for Lissenberg, I think.'

'And she will sing – for Lissenberg – at my party?'

'Oh, she'll sing. She's a professional. Mademoiselle de Beauharnais wants the duets from *Night of Errors*.'

'I suppose we have to have the husband too?'

'Oh, I think so.' Something made her absolutely certain that he knew of the separation that had taken place between Cristabel and Fylde. Well, of course he did. He was formidably well informed.

'But not in *Night of Errors*?'

'Don't you think that opera – and how Prince Gustav tried to use it – is best forgotten?'

'Yes. Such a pity! Because what Lady Cristabel managed to do with that inferior bit of work was amazing. But I have something that I hope will prove really worthy of her.'

'Oh?'

'I found it yesterday, hidden among Prince Gustav's papers. Would you believe it? The young composer Beethoven sent in an opera to the Lissenberg contest last year and Prince Gustav chose to suppress it.'

'Good gracious! And never said a word? But why?'

'Characteristic. Herr van Beethoven had left out the essential element of flattery.' His smile was very friendly. 'I confess I long to know how your husband was persuaded to put in his prologue to *Crusader Prince*.'

'Not by me.' She smiled too, remembering how Franz had had to explain it to her. 'He knew he had to win, you see.'

'His was a clever choice of subject, mind you. Gustav was bound to identify with the gallant Saint Brandt, and would not have noticed a little thing like his ill-treatment of his wife. Beethoven's subject was not nearly so tactful, but I think Lady Cristabel will like it. It's a political tragedy, the story of Regulus. Do you know it?'

'A Roman general? Something about Carthage?'

'That's the one. The Carthaginians took him prisoner, sent him back to Rome on parole to offer peace terms. When he got there, he urged the Romans not to make peace, then refused to breach his parole and went back to torture and certain death.'

'A strong story! I think I can see why Herr van Beethoven didn't think it suitable for Vienna. Sent it here instead. But what part would Cristabel play?'

'There's a devoted page, Marcus. In love with Regulus' daughter Livia, but loving Regulus still more. Even Regulus urges Marcus to stay in Rome, to live and marry Livia. Marcus won't do it. There's a tremendous duet about honour; her and Regulus at the end. You can imagine the kind of thing. As she will sing it, it should bring the house down. I thought, if she only agrees, we might have her sing that at our party. Will you ask her, please, for me?'

'Would it not be better to do it yourself?'

'You are absolutely right. But – she's a great lady as well as a great singer. I am afraid to ask her to come and see me, in case she refuses.'

'She even might.' Martha thought about it. 'Would you like me to invite her up to the palace tomorrow? Once she's here, it will be easier for you to ask to see her.'

'If you would. And without the husband, if you can.'

'I can try. And even if he should come, which he is entirely capable of doing, there is nothing to stop you playing the tyrant and insisting on seeing her alone.'

'I don't believe I'd play the tyrant very well.'

'No, neither do I.' She smiled at him, surprised at finding herself so entirely his friend.

Martha's messenger found Cristabel alone at the hostel next day, since things were still very much at sixes and sevens at the opera house and Fylde had gone down to Lissenberg on some vague errand that would doubtless end up at the gaming table.

'Princess Martha wants to see me,' Cristabel told her aunt.

'I'm glad. I must confess to being devoured with curiosity as to how they are going on up at the palace.'

'Would you like to come too?'

'Not if I am not asked, my dear. I suspect that Martha has quite enough on her hands in dealing with Minette de Beauharnais. And she'll be missing Count Tafur, I am sure.'

'We all are.' She moved over to look out of the window. 'It almost looks like snow. They are beginning to clear out the tunnel, did you know, getting ready for winter?'

'So soon?'

'Yes. They must expect an early winter.'

'They are probably wrong,' said Lady Helen comfortably. 'Weather prophets usually seem to be.'

'Pity it isn't snowing,' Cristabel had been following her own train of thought. 'Then I could go up through the tunnel, quite informally and be certain of seeing Martha alone, as I am sure she wishes.'

'Best not, don't you think?' said her aunt. 'The first time you call at the palace under its new regime.'

'New regime! Its usurper, you mean. Its tyrant!'

'Tyrant? Prince Joseph is hardly behaving like one, by all the reports one hears.'

'Oh, reports! Set forward by himself, no doubt. I just hope, aunt, that I am not so unfortunate as to meet him. I'm not at all sure I would be able to keep a civil tongue in my head.'

'Dear child, do, pray, be careful.' Lady Helen was seriously concerned now. 'Don't let your old friendship for the two princes betray you into any foolishness . . .'

'Oh, I won't, aunt, I promise I won't. I'll even do my level best to be civil to Minette if I should meet her.' Now she produced a bitter travesty of a laugh. 'If I wasn't so angry with Prince Joseph I could almost be sorry for him. How long do you think before the announcement, aunt? A week? A month? Or – ' a new thought struck her. 'Do you think her uncle the all-powerful Emperor left her here to choose between the two available princes? If she should decide she preferred Max after all, would he be handed Lissenberg, do you think?'

'Cristabel!' Now Lady Helen was both shocked and anxious. 'You cannot still be thinking about Prince Max? Don't forget – '

'That I'm a married lady? I never forget that. How could I, so fortunate as my marriage has turned out.'

'Oh, my dear.' Suddenly, appallingly, Lady Helen was in tears. 'I'll never forgive myself.'

'Ah, don't!' Cristabel amazed herself by hugging her formidable aunt. 'It's nobody's fault but mine. Don't make it harder for me to forgive myself.'

'And him?'

'Who? Oh – Desmond! I try not to think about him. But I must not keep Martha waiting.'

'Give her my love.'

'I will. And don't fret, aunt. What's done, is done. We must just live with it as best we can, and I do bless you for the help you are giving me.'

'You look well!' Cristabel had been glad to find Martha still in the royal apartments. After the first embrace, she held her friend at arm's length to look at her. 'I've never seen you in such a glow! You thrive on deposition?'

'Do you know, we do!' Martha only wished she could return the compliment, but thought Cristabel looked wretched.

'Franz too?'

'Why, yes, I think so. You know what it's been like for him, this last year. He's done his best, and small thanks he's had for it. Now, he's a free man again, doing the work he loves. And, Cristabel, we all like Joseph so much!'

'How can you!'

'It's rather, how can we not?'

'Napoleon's spy! When I think how he wormed his way in . . . Opened the gates of Lissenberg to the tyrant!'

'Well, Cristabel, hardly that. It was actually my poor Franz who showed Napoleon the way to take Lissenberg. Just think how much worse things might have been for us all, if it had not been for Joseph.'

'Does he call you Martha?'

'Yes.'

'I don't understand you! And I suppose, the next thing, you will be welcoming Minette de Beauharnais as a sister-in-law?'

'Ah, now that is a question, isn't it? Franz thinks so, but, for myself, I'm not so sure. But – ' with a glance at the clock on the chimney piece, 'Cristabel, I've a confession to make to you. I have got you here on false pretences. Joseph asked me to. He wants to see you. He has a favour to ask of you.'

'A favour? Of me?' Her eyes showed brilliant in a blanched face. 'And if I refuse to see him?'

'Please don't do that, Cristabel. For all our sakes?'

*

Introduced by Baron Hals, Cristabel found Joseph kneeling on the floor of his study, measuring something on an enormous map. He folded it with a swift movement, rose to his feet, held out both hands. 'Lady Cristabel! Forgive me?'

She ignored the appealing hands, swept him an almost theatrical curtsy. 'What is there for me to forgive, if your brothers have? And Martha. They are your relations, I am merely your paid entertainer. You have something to add, perhaps, to Mademoiselle de Beauharnais's instructions about the entertainment for her party?'

'Instructions?'

'What else? She quite longs to hear the final duet from *Night of Errors*.' Even through her anger, the parody of Minette's fluting tones came over, clear and sardonic.

'Intolerable! I never meant . . . I've wished so much to thank you for *Crusader Prince* – for what you did for my brothers. And for Lissenberg. You stood between Lissenberg and disaster.'

'No need to thank me, prince. I did it for Lissenberg, not for any of you. And I enjoyed doing it.'

'So brilliantly! Must you be so formal with me? I had hoped we were friends.'

'I thought we were. I also thought you were Doctor Joseph. I must congratulate you on your brilliant coup, highness. And on your approaching marriage?'

'No! There are limits to what I will do, even for Lissenberg.'

'You'll marry her to poor Max then? Demand from him the sacrifice you won't make yourself?'

'Cristabel!' Once again his hand went out, looking for hers, but she had withdrawn a swift step.

'Lady Cristabel! No: Mrs Desmond Fylde!' Her colour was high now, her eyes sparkling with rage.

'I wish you would sit down! That's what I wanted to talk to you about. Your marriage. I have undertaken to introduce Napoleon's legal code without delay. You will be able to obtain a divorce, and I urge that you do so as soon as possible.'

'How good of you to interest yourself in my affairs!' She had taken another step away from him. 'And now, if you will permit, I must return to my duties. I promise you that

Mademoiselle de Beauharnais will not be disappointed next week, though I confess I am surprised that you approve her choice of music.'

'But I don't! That's the other thing I want to tell you.' And, feeling himself almost babbling, he plunged into a description of the Beethoven opera he had found. It won him her professional attention at least, and she showed the first sign of warmth when he handed her copies he had had made of the duet between Regulus and Marcus.

'Thank you.' She was still standing. 'I promise I'll do my best – we'll do our best, my husband and I. For Lissenberg. For a quiet winter.'

'Not for me?'

'Why in the world should I do anything for you?'

14

The day before the party, a mud-stained messenger brought the news that Napoleon had taken Ulm and was poised to attack Vienna. 'You see!' Minette told Martha. 'He is carrying all before him as usual, that amazing uncle of mine. If only we get the news of Vienna's fall before winter seals the roads! It would immensely strengthen dear Joseph's position. What a glutton for work that man is! It's harder to gain access to him than to the Emperor himself. I think we should explain to him, Martha dear, that there is more to governing a country than paperwork. He won't make himself loved here in Lissenberg if he's always too busy to see people.'

'He made a special journey to Brundt to deliver the invitations to your party in person,' Martha pointed out. 'And so far as I know everyone is coming.'

'Every single kraut and burgher!' Minette had not liked seeing what she had meant as a select little party so extended. 'How in the world are you going to fit them all in, Martha?'

'By opening up the armoury on one side of the great hall, and the guard-room on the other.' Martha smiled. 'I've had to borrow all the tapestries from the opera house and the hostel, and Frau Schmidt has promised to come early and bring me some from Brundt. We'll have refreshments in the armoury, dancing in the great hall, with the orchestra on the dais. And the singers there too, of course.'

'This mysterious Beethoven opera that everyone's so excited about. I never could endure his music myself, but I suppose one must sit through it out of courtesy to Cristabel. But, Martha, the dancing. That ridiculous man Joseph is so busy . . . Has he thought that he must open the ball? Suitably partnered – ' A significant pause.

'I expect so,' said Martha. 'But you know, Minette, he's been so absorbed since the Emperor's engineers arrived that

146

there has been no getting him to think about anything else. When I ask about the party, he just leaves everything to me!'

'But he sees you!' Minette pounced on it.

'Five minutes every morning. Question and answer, and he's off to the mountains again with the engineers. They want to ride both ends of the cut they plan before winter closes in; and the country is pretty rugged, he says. He's enjoying himself!' It was impossible not to like Joseph for the way he had plunged into this arduous work, and it was doing him good, she thought. Tanned and toughened by the all-weather riding, he no longer looked so much older than his brothers.

'Oh, men!' said Minette. 'Well, tomorrow morning, Martha, you remind him about opening the ball! It won't do to get the Lissenbergers together and then affront them by any breach of ceremony.'

'No.' Martha agreed. 'But then, there are all kinds of ways to affront people, aren't there? It's not going to be an easy occasion, Minette. I just hope it isn't a disastrous one.'

'Krauts and burghers,' said Minette again. 'What they need is a lavish show, and I am sure we can rely on you to provide that, Martha. What a good creature you are, to be sure, to take so much trouble for the man who has ousted your husband. I do hope you realise how much we appreciate it, even if my wicked Joseph is too busy to say so.'

'I hope you won't treat our guests as "krauts and burghers", Minette.'

'I suppose you think I should dance with your dear friend Ishmael Brodski, just to show what good democrats we are.'

'If he were to ask you,' said Martha.

Desmond Fylde was finding Beethoven's music hard to sing, as indeed it was, but worth it, in Cristabel's opinion, which he did not share. Franz kept them late at the opera house on the night before the party and had a qualm of conscience when he finally let them go. Cristabel looked exhausted, and Fylde looked predatory. But he was already overdue at the palace, where, he knew, there were a million things still to be done.

'Rest well,' he told Cristabel. 'I'm sure it will go brilliantly tomorrow. And then we can get down to work on the opera itself. Exactly what we need for this winter.'

'Not a call to revolution in it anywhere?'

'No. Just love of country. What could be more suitable for Lissenberg right now?'

'And love of one another,' said Cristabel. 'Regulus may love Rome, but Marcus loves Regulus.'

'Hard on Livia,' said Fylde, and it came back to Franz that during the day he had seen some kind of angry exchange between Fylde and Maria, the seconda donna who sang Livia. 'And hard, too,' Fylde went on, 'that Maria is not to sing tomorrow. Can I not persuade you to change your mind about that?'

'I'm afraid not.' Maria sang Beethoven's difficult music even worse than Fylde, but one could hardly tell him that. 'The prince has asked that the entertainment be kept short, as you know, leaving plenty of time for talk and dancing. You two are just the appetiser to the feast.'

'What a vulgarian!' Fylde had firmly taken Cristabel's arm as they left the opera house. 'Lissenberg's well rid of him. The appetiser indeed! And all this talk about love of country is quite comic, when you think about our Doctor – Prince Joseph, born in Switzerland, bred in France, a man out for himself if ever there was one. He loves Lissenberg the way a gourmet loves a truffle. To swallow it whole.' His pressure on her arm increased. 'That's one opinion we share, you and I, as I well know. Scorn for the interloper who made such a public fool of you. Doctor Joseph indeed! Pretender and mountebank. It makes me mad to remember how I let him pull the wool over my eyes! Left him alone to "examine" you. We could make things very awkward for Prince Joseph if we were so minded, you and I.'

'What in the world do you mean?' They had reached the main hall of the hostel and she turned to face him, withdrawing her arm from his.

'Pretending to be a doctor! Interfering between man and wife! Oh, I've held my tongue for your sake, my queen, but much more of this high-handed behaviour and I shall feel moved to speak.'

'What high-handed behaviour?'

'Making us sing this trash of Beethoven's! And then leaving poor Maria out of it. She feels it, poor girl, she feels it badly.'

'So badly that she has taken up with a French officer.' She regretted the words as soon as they were spoken.

'Well, poor girl, how could she hope to hold me when everyone knows my heart is yours? Always has been, always will. We have to talk, my own, and not here in public. I've heard from Vienna at last. A firm offer. For the two of us! We can wash our hands of Lissenberg.'

'Vienna?' She was so surprised that she let him follow her into her own apartments. 'But Napoleon will be there any day now!'

'What's that to the purpose? I'd sing for the devil himself, if he would just get me out of Lissenberg.'

'You've been gambling! You're in debt!' They were not questions.

'Oh, my angel, nothing to signify. But I have realised something, understood something at last. There is no hope for us, for you and me, here in Lissenberg. Oh, I don't blame you, how should I, for having regal memories, letting them maybe grow into hopes. Two unmarried princes, and everyone knows one of them adored you once. But you married me, remember. And you had better remember, and show it, or I could make bad trouble – and not just for you.'

'I wouldn't try it, if I were you.' She was white with anger. 'I have friends here in Lissenberg, and some standing. And Prince Joseph has absolute power. Just think about that, before you make your filthy suggestions about him. Martha and I spent a night, once, in the cells below the palace. Oh, they let us off lightly. We sat with the guards by their fire, but it is not a night I shall forget. Your voice, what remains of it, would not last long if you were to find yourself shut up in the dungeons themselves.'

'You wouldn't – '

'It's not what I would do. It is what Prince Joseph would. It has been a brilliant, bloodless coup so far and he is working hard to keep it that way. But don't think he might not be savage, if challenged.'

149

'You helped him to it. I'll never understand that, not so long as I live.'

'I don't suppose you will. I'm not sure I do myself. But it had to be done. I knew that, if I knew nothing else. Otherwise I truly think the opera house would have run red with Lissenberg blood that night. And it would have ended with Lissenberg absorbed totally into France, instead of the fragile independence we still have.'

'Good gracious.' Mocking. 'You sound like a Lissenberger, my angel.'

'I feel like a Lissenberger. And I am not your angel. Once and for all, I ask you to recognise that I no longer look on you as my husband, except in the most pettifogging legal sense. Half my earnings, yes. Any part of my life, never.' She moved across the room, to the door that led to Lady Helen's room. 'Now, do I call Aunt Helen and the servants, and have you forcibly removed, or will you try to behave like a gentleman, and go?'

'Oh, I'll go where I'm wanted, never fear for that. And I won't come back.'

'Except to sing with me, I trust.'

'With what remains of my voice? You wouldn't prefer to have one of those out-of-work princes sing with you instead? You were getting on famously with Prince Franz, I remember, when I came here last year. And then there's your old love, who let you steal his laurels all that time ago, Prince Max. A pity they're such a starchy lot here in Lissenberg, or I'd seriously consider letting you make it worth my while to help you to a divorce, now that we're in for French law here. But it would be no use, would it, my poor angel, no use at all?'

'You make me sick,' she said.

It was snowing a little on the morning of the party, light scurries of flakes blowing against the palace windows, and Martha paused anxiously from time to time in the course of her preparations to peer out of a window and wonder if the Lissenbergers would make this their excuse not to come. She had invited Frau Schmidt to stay at the palace, but the old lady had sent a friendly note to say she had already arranged to spend the night with friends in Lissenberg. Implicit in it was the knowledge that if she came to the party, her friends must come too. Minette's party would only be a good idea if everyone came, and would they? And what would happen if they did? Prince Joseph had arranged that no French soldiers should be in sight, though they would naturally be on call in their barracks below the castle. And their officers had had to be invited. What might the volatile Lissenbergers do if they were to feel themselves the overwhelming majority? Or if trouble broke out with the French officers, who did tend to behave like lords of creation?

Martha put this to Franz as they were dressing for the party, and he shook his head at her. 'Don't even think about it. But if anything should happen, remember that I trust Joseph absolutely.'

'I'm glad,' she said. 'So do I.'

Minette had not been pleased when Joseph made it clear that Martha must stand with him to receive their guests, and was even less so when she discovered that he was to open the dancing with Frau Schmidt. She sulked through the reception, only coming to life when she found herself sitting beside Joseph in the crowded hall, waiting for Cristabel to sing. There was a slight delay, and she turned restlessly to look back at the hall and whisper to Joseph, 'They've come, every man jack of them. I knew it was a good idea.'

'Yes,' he said quietly. 'I'm grateful to you. Ah!' Franz had appeared on the dais.

He raised a hand for silence and the crowded hall stilled. 'I am grieved to tell you that Herr Fylde, who should have sung Regulus, is indisposed. My brother, Prince Max, has gallantly agreed to take his part at short notice, and begs your tolerance while he does his best with Herr van Beethoven's remarkable music. As you all doubtless remember, he and Lady Cristabel have sung together before, many years ago.' This got a roar of friendly appreciation from the audience, as he turned to welcome Cristabel and Max on to the dais.

'Well!' said Minette. 'There's a new come on!'

'Hush!' said Joseph.

Max stepped forward to tell the audience, briefly, about the opera and its theme. 'Lady Cristabel has done me the great honour,' he concluded, 'of letting me sing the last duet with her. It is sung before Regulus and his devoted page go off to meet their death together. Death for their country. Before we sing it, Lady Cristabel has asked me to say to you that she, personally, still thinks it preferable to live for one's country.' His hand stilled the little murmur of appreciation. 'Now!' He turned to Franz, at the fortepiano.

When it ended, Martha was crying. She thought most people were. Even Minette, on the other side of Joseph, had a hand up to her eyes. And the applause contrived to be both enthusiastic and yet, somehow, muted.

'What a woman!' Joseph turned to Minette. 'She holds us in the hollow of her hand.'

'Except her husband,' said Minette. 'He's here, I notice. Too ill to sing but not to dance.' The musicians were filing on to the dais and Joseph moved away with an apology to find Frau Schmidt. Left alone, Minette looked angrily around. Max was preparing to dance with Cristabel, and Franz with Martha. Intolerable to think she might find herself partnerless. Baron Hals was moving towards her through the crowd. To take pity on her himself? Or to propose some 'suitable' Lissenberger? She looked about for a French officer.

'Madame!' Desmond Fylde appeared beside her. 'Will you do me the honour? My wife prefers a prince to her husband. Will you let me take my revenge by dancing with the most elegant young lady in the room? We'll show these clods of Lissenbergers what dancing really is!'

'In a polonaise?' But she took his hand. 'I suppose Prince Joseph chose the dull dance in respect for his partner's advancing years.'

'Even in a polonaise you will shine as always; a little glimpse of civilisation in this barbarous country. It has been my pleasure to watch you from afar, to admire the grace with which you bear the clumsy attentions of the princes. What did you think of Prince Max's performance just now?'

'I thought he sang like a prince.'

152

'Excellent!' He pressed her hand. 'Just like a prince! I tremble to think what is going to happen to our gallant little opera company this winter, with two amateur princes in charge. I hope to persuade my wife that we should leave before the snow comes. This music of van Beethoven's is not at all what she should be singing. I am afraid she may damage her voice if she persists in doing so, and we have the most pressing offers from Vienna, where, I imagine, we will have the honour of entertaining that great man, your uncle, the Emperor. I was desolated not to have the pleasure of meeting him when he paid his remarkable flying visit to Lissenberg. As an Irish prince, I think I could have given him some useful advice about an approach to my country that might get him the base he needs for an attack on the great enemy, England. I am sure that with my friends to prepare the ground he would find himself welcomed as an ally in the struggle for Irish independence.'

'Good gracious!' They had made one full circle of the hall now in the slow movement of the stately dance, and she hesitated, pausing imperceptibly by the entrance to the guard-room. 'An Irish prince?'

'Why should you know, since here I am treated merely as a poor brute of a singer? My wife is Lady Cristabel, but who would think of giving me my title?' He bent over her, dark eyes flashing. 'I am descended, lady, from Cuchulainn, the great hero, the Hound of Ulster. But what does the English oppressor care about that? I am heir to mile upon mile of fertile Irish soil, and look at me! Earning a miserable wage as a professional entertainer. Despised, I have to face it, even by my English wife. It was not I, milady, who declared myself unable to perform today. She decided she would prefer to sing with a prince!' As he talked, he had guided her out of the circle of dance and into a quiet corner of the armoury. 'But, forgive me, I am talking too much of myself. Tell me how you endure the tedium of life here in Lissenberg, the prospect of being shut up here for the winter with only our so gallant princes for company? It will be a sad change, I am afraid, from the pleasures of Paris.'

'It will indeed.' She agreed wholeheartedly. 'But as a prince yourself sir, you will understand the duties of rank. My uncle has left me here as his representative; he counts on me to watch his interests here.'

'And more than that.' He gave a quick conspiratorial look round, bent close, to speak low. 'He means you to bind the prince – one of the princes – to him by marriage. What a wickedness! What a sacrifice! Your elegance, your brains, your beauty thrown away on a boor who doesn't even have the intelligence to appreciate you. Hush!' He silenced her angry protest. 'Everyone knows that Prince Max has loved my wife from childhood, hopelessly, romantically, idiotically. Fewer people know that she has entangled Joseph too in her wiles. You probably don't know the story – why should you? But when he was posing as a doctor, spying on Lissenberg, before you came, he persuaded Prince Franz to let him visit my wife. She was having a little trouble with her voice, you understand. It enrages me to remember that I let him talk me into allowing him to see her alone. What went on between them I shall never know. I prefer not even to think about it! I am a much ill used man. Only my pride holds me up. At first, it would not let me tell you this, expose my own shame to you, but then, seeing you so beautiful, so brave – so monstrously deceived, how could I not speak?'

'Prince Joseph? And your wife? I don't believe it!'

'Open your eyes, madame, and you will. But I have monopolised you for too long. Forgive me, and remember that there is one man in Lissenberg who would risk death to serve you.'

'It's going to work.' Ishmael Brodski had asked Martha to dance with him, but she had suggested that they stand and watch instead. 'That's a remarkable man, Prince Joseph,' Brodski went on. 'Will you forgive me if I tell you I think he will make a better Prince of Lissenberg than either of his delightful brothers?'

'Indeed I will.' Smiling at him. 'I think so too, and so, I suspect do his brothers. But I'm surprised as well as delighted to see that Lissenberg seems to agree. The attendance tonight is surely a very cheering vote of confidence. Don't you think?'

'I do indeed.' He smiled down at her from his handsome height. 'You're a remarkable woman, if I may say so as an old friend. Your quiet support of Prince Joseph has meant a great deal to the Lissenbergers.'

'To the women,' she said. 'But I am specially pleased to see so many people from Brundt.'

'Right to be.' He turned to peer out into the darkening day. 'Snowing again. That's good.'

'Good? I'm afraid it may mean a difficult journey for you back to Brundt.'

'But not impossible. Whereas I begin to hope that the pass to Lake Constance is going to be closed earlier than usual this year.'

'You're looking forward to that?' A little shiver ran down her spine. 'I hate the feeling of being shut in here. Please God this will be the last year of it, if Prince Joseph's new road goes on as well next year as he hopes.'

'They have started blasting today.' He had gently manoeuvred her so that she had her back to the window and he stood between her and the room. Now he leaned down to speak close to her ear. 'We all know in Brundt. No way of keeping it dark. It's not the road Napoleon expected at all.'

'What do you mean?'

'I thought you didn't know. I imagine Prince Joseph wants to spare his brothers the dangerous knowledge as long as possible. But everyone knows in Brundt. It's time you did too.'

'What are you saying?' She gave a quick look round, but the orchestra was playing a loud and lively gigue and there seemed no chance of being overheard.

'That Napoleon assumed the new road would go by the line of the secret way; across the mountains; down to the Danube and so into the territory of his new allies. And water transport down the Danube for the dangerous products of Brundt, all ready for a campaign in the east.'

'And it's not?'

'No. Joseph and his engineers have found quite another route, south and west from Brundt. He's Swiss, remember. The road will end in Switzerland.'

'A country that always tries to be neutral.'

'Just so.'

'Napoleon will be furious.'

'Precisely. Now you understand why I want an early winter.'

'So he doesn't learn until it is too late. But if everyone in Brundt knows?'

'They won't tell. The French officers don't know. It's a remarkable conspiracy of silence. But this party is an extra hazard . . .'

'It seemed such a good idea.' She put a hand to her head, suddenly dizzy.

'You're not well!' His quick hand steadied her as she swayed on her feet.

'It's nothing! Hot in here . . . Some air?' Even with her head swimming, she was amused to see that he knew the way to the little side door that led on to a terrace. 'Thank you! The cold air's all I need.' She stood for a moment, breathing it in, grateful for his supporting arm. 'You're a good friend,' she said at last.

'I love you,' he said. 'You know that. Always have, always will. And I think I am to congratulate you? And your husband?'

'I do begin to think so.' She smiled in the darkness. 'But it is our secret for the moment, dear friend.'

'And shall remain so. Your husband has not noticed?'

'They are all so busy! But, this road! I'm glad Lodge and Playfair are gone! It's the kind of secret they would have been happy to sell to the highest bidder. Prince Gustav is under close guard; no danger there. And you think the Lissenbergers . . .'

'Are united, for once, and long may it last. It's the French officers I worry about. And Herr Fylde.'

'Ah.' She thought about it. 'Yes. But he's tied to the money Lady Cristabel can earn him. And she has promised me she will stay here.'

'I'm glad to hear it. That's a weight off my mind. Do you feel better?'

'Yes, thank you. And,' smiling up at him, 'you are quite right. We really should not be lingering here any longer.

I do thank you, my good friend. And – shall I tell my husband?'

'I'm sure you should tell him everything.'

'You *are* a good friend.' She let him lead her back into the crowded room.

'Our dance at last!' Minette de Beauharnais greeted Joseph as she turned from a quick word with the leader of the small orchestra. 'I have waited for this moment all evening, but I must congratulate you on your duty well and truly done. It's going brilliantly, don't you think?'

'Yes, brilliantly. It's snowing again,' and then, as she showed her surprise at the apparent irrelevance, he said, 'Good gracious! A waltz!'

'I asked for it.' With what was intended as her most ravishing smile. 'I did not want our French guests to think us quite barbarous, here in Lissenberg.'

'The officers, you mean.' It had gone against the grain with him that they had to be invited.

'Such a gallant band of men, resigning themselves to their winter of exile. We must do all we can to make it tolerable for them.'

'And you?' he asked. 'Are you sure you do not regret exiling yourself here, if that is what you feel about it?'

'How could I?' She seemed to melt in his arms. 'When my heart is here?'

'Oh, my dear lady.' He took her in a swoop across the hall, wryly amused to see his way clear. 'Are you telling me that you have lost your heart to my brother Max? As your good friend and your uncle's ally, I must warn you that Max still wears the willow for his old love, Lady Cristabel. He never means to marry.'

'Max!' She said angrily. 'What has Max to do with anything? It was not for Max's sake that my uncle brought me here.'

He took her another vigorous turn of the room, letting the awkward silence lengthen on this declaration. Then: 'Do you know,' he said, 'it is snowing harder now? As your uncle's friend, and, I hope, yours, I think I should urge you to make your escape from dull little Lissenberg while it is still possible.'

'You are asking me to leave?' Now she was rigid in his arms.

'Far from it. It is a delight to have you here, and, I know, a great pleasure for my sister Martha, but it is asking too much, it seems to me, to expect you to waste your charms on us, when conquered Vienna awaits you.' They had passed close to the musicians as he spoke, and a small imperative gesture brought the music to a swirling climax. He took her once more across the hall to where he saw Martha standing with Ishmael Brodski, let her go and bent over her hand. 'My deepest thanks for a delightful dance.' He turned to Martha. 'You look tired, my dear, come and sit this one out with me.'

'Madame – ' Brodski was embarking on the inevitable offer when Desmond Fylde appeared at his side.

'Our dance, I think.' He held out an imperative hand to Minette, who took it, still speechless with rage and shock at Joseph's rejection. The musicians were playing a minuet now and Fylde kept the conversation to a social minimum for a while to let her recover her temper, then suggested that they move to the armoury for a glass of wine. 'You have been dancing without a pause all evening, as I have cause to know, having followed your every step. And I am afraid that perhaps Prince Joseph has said something you did not quite like. I told you the man was a boor.'

'He suggested I leave! Too kind! For my own sake, of course.' She drank eagerly of the sparkling wine. 'It's snowing, he says.'

'Yes, hard. The road will be closed soon. You can have no idea what it is like here in the winter. However insulting, Prince Joseph gave you good advice. Now, listen to me, madame.' Once more, he had contrived to find them a secluded corner. 'I have learned something, since we talked before. By merest chance, I overheard a conversation – something your uncle would give a great deal to know. To know now, not next spring. You understand me?'

'Not precisely.' She finished her wine.

'A dangerous secret. I'll not burden you with it, but I promise you, help me get it to your uncle, and he'll forgive you any little matrimonial disappointment. No, rather, he will congratulate you on your wisdom in refusing the advances of his unfaithful ally.'

'Unfaithful? Of course! That explains everything. Very well, I'll do it. But, how? When?'

'Tomorrow,' he said. 'Listen carefully.'

15

'You're leaving today?' Martha had wakened feeling sick and fragile after her late night at the party and been far from pleased at Minette's demand for an early interview, but this was news indeed. 'You've seen Prince Joseph?'

'No.' Carelessly. 'Nor mean to, since he was already off to the mountains when I asked for a farewell interview. You – so publicly his right hand – will do just as well. Better! Tell him from me that I can take a hint when it is thrown in my face.'

'But may he not have messages for your uncle? For the Emperor?'

'If he has, he can send them after me. Have you looked out your window? It's snowing hard this morning. If I am to be over the pass before it closes, I must leave at once. I've ordered my carriage; I leave in half an hour; you will say my farewells to your husband and Prince Max. And to Cristabel, of course. And I wish you joy of the winter here, Martha.'

'But, Minette, is it safe? You must take a Lissenberg guide, in case the pass is blocked already. Have you sent to have the road checked?' Martha wished desperately that she did not feel so ill.

'Of course I have. Don't fuss, Martha dear. I know what I'm doing. Just think! I might even catch up with my uncle in time to ride in to Vienna at his side.'

'But will he not be angry if he meant you to stay?' Martha was remembering Minette's high colour and look of suppressed anger after her dance with Joseph the night before. What had happened between them? She had thought it none of her business at the time, now she was not so sure.

'On the contrary, I promise you my uncle will be delighted to see me! And hear all my news! Goodbye, dear Martha. I am sad to part with *you*. I'll think of you this winter, when I am dancing at the Hofburg. And you shall hear from me in the spring, when the roads are open.'

Was it a promise or a threat? Left alone, Martha was miserably doubtful about this. Should she let Minette go? How could she have stopped her? She must send to Franz at the opera house. In a moment. Right now, she felt worse than ever. Ring for Anna. She rose, took a dizzy step and felt blackness closing in.

Minette's servants were glad to leave, and worked with a will. The carriage was ready only a little late, and she herself only a little later than that. There was no sign of further objection from Martha, and she would not let Baron Hals delay her with his protests. Once again she refused the offer of a Lissenberg guide. 'Ridiculous. My people know the way. The snow has stopped; the road is reported open. My uncle will not thank you if you delay me and I am benighted as a result.'

It was a clinching argument. Hals bowed and stood back to watch anxiously as Minette followed her maid into the heavy carriage. Then, at the last moment, he moved forward to hold the door. 'Prince Joseph. Your farewell message?'

'I gave it to Princess Martha.' She and her maid were both wrapped in enormous fur cloaks so that he could not see beyond them into the carriage. 'But you may say "*Auf wiedersehen*" to the prince for me, if you will. Drive on coachman.'

'Phew!' Desmond Fylde rose from the well of the coach when they were out of sight of the castle. 'I thought I'd stifle in there while the old mountebank kept you talking. I liked your farewell message. "*Auf wiedersehen*" indeed! You expect to see the prince in chains in Vienna?'

'I'd be happy to. Now, we must lose no time.' Minette was enjoying herself. 'Tilde,' she said to her maid. 'The cloak, please.' And, as the girl handed it to Fylde, revealing herself warmly dressed in men's clothes: 'It had better be outside for you right away, Tilde, just in case Prince Joseph has guards on the road. Better safe than sorry, and you know I'll make it worth your while.'

'Oh, I don't mind,' said the girl cheerfully. 'I've a score to settle with Louis the coachman.' She pulled the check string and when the carriage slowed to a halt got nimbly out, exchanged a couple of pleasantries with the two men up behind and climbed on to the box with the coachman.

'You should be one of your uncle's marshals,' said Fylde admiringly as the carriage moved slowly forward. 'It's all gone as smoothly as this?'

'Yes. But we're later than I meant. I had to wait until all three princes had left the palace before breaking my news to Martha. I thought for a moment I was going to have trouble with her. Lord, she takes herself seriously, that one. But, you? You got off without rousing suspicion?'

'No trouble at all.' He did not explain that he had spent the night with Maria, simply not returned to the hostel before coming up to the palace to seize his chance and smuggle himself into her carriage. 'But I am afraid I shall have to be dependent on you for funds, just at first. There was no way I could get to the strong box without my careful wife suspecting something. But I promise you, the news I bring your uncle will be worth a princedom to him.'

'Lissenberg, you mean? Now we are safe away, do tell me what it is?'

'Dear lady, not yet! Not while we are still within Prince Joseph's territory. We might be stopped by his guards; you must know nothing for your own sweet sake. And, just in case – ' He laid the maid's big cloak handy beside him in the seat. 'Hooded, I see. What a conspirator you are! The slightest hint of danger and I am your devoted maidservant, swathed to the ears against the toothache. Your servants won't blab, I take it.'

'They know their place better than that. Lord, it's cold! Pass me your hot brick and pull the rug around me.'

He had promised himself that he would go slowly with Minette. After all, the journey, in this weather, must last several days, there was plenty of time to woo and win her before the confrontation with Napoleon. But her careless tone, almost as if to a servant, acted as the kind of challenge he could not resist. 'I'll do better than that, my lovely!' He reached down to move his own hot brick under her feet, then swooped on her, rug and all, to gather her in his arms. 'Two are always warmer than one. What is it?'

162

She had eluded him, withdrawn to the far corner of the carriage. 'So, I was right to think a little about you! I asked a few questions about you last night. Don't come nearer! I'll pull the check string if you do. Have them throw you out into the snow.'

'You wouldn't!'

'Don't try me! I thought I'd give you a chance. If you were to behave like a gentleman as far as the frontier, I'd take you with me. If not, I'd hand you over to the guards there, tell them you had stowed away in my carriage. You surely did not think I would not know what happened to Cristabel? How you blackmailed her into marriage. Well, you won't do that to me!'

'No, dear lady,' he managed to collect himself a little, 'since I'm married to Cristabel. We must be friends, you and I, or we could do each other great harm. Forgive me if I overstepped the mark just now; blame your own charms. How can I help but adore you!' He too had withdrawn to his own corner of the carriage and was thinking desperately. Fool, idiot, to have been so sure of Minette. Had he really thrown away the lifetime security of marriage to Cristabel for a will-o'-the-wisp – a dream of a quick divorce and marriage to Napoleon's powerful niece?

'As you adore so many others. Let's forget that side of it, shall we, and talk like the pair of conspirators we are. Tell me what this secret is you have for my uncle and I'll turn the carriage round, take you down close enough to the castle for safety and leave you there. Make up your mind. I must not risk more delay.'

'Go back there? I can't do it!' He did not believe this was happening to him.

'Burned your boats, have you?' Not a trace of sympathy in her tone. 'That's your problem.'

'Just take me with you as far as the frontier,' he begged. 'I'll tell you then; trouble you no further.' He had a horrible vision of struggling back to the castle through the thickening snow, arriving bedraggled: the talk, the laughter, the questions.

'No,' she said. 'How can I trust you not to play the same game with me as you did with Cristabel? You never thought she was my friend, did you?' And then, surprised. 'Well, nor did I. Or Martha. But I find that they are. And you, Mr Fylde, are contemptible. Now, time's passing. Make up your mind.'

'Bitch!' Fatally, totally, he lost his temper, lunged at her. 'You led me on. I'll make you sorry.' But she had reached for the check string; the carriage juddered to a halt. The two men perched behind were so quick to the doors that he realised, in so far as he was capable of realising anything, that they must have had orders to be ready.

'Throw him out,' she told the two men.

'No! Dear lady! You can't! We're at the top of the pass.'

'Not quite,' she said implacably. 'It will be a healthy walk for you, Mr Fylde.'

'No! Wait! I'll tell you – '

'Too late. Get rid of him,' she told the men. 'He's a coward; don't hurt him.' And, to the coachman. 'Drive on.'

'Martha!' Franz's voice came to her as from a great distance. 'My darling! Wake up! Look at me!'

It was an effort to open her eyes. Franz was holding her hand, Anna beside him with smelling salts. Something was terribly wrong. 'I'm all right.' She pressed his hand reassuringly, felt the warm instant response. 'But, how long? What's happened?'

'Anna found you; luckily I'd just come back. What did Minette do to you, my darling?'

'Nothing. That's it! She came to say goodbye. Has she gone? It's not safe, over the mountains without a guide. I was going for help. Oh, don't worry about me. Go quick, see if she's gone. Anna will look after me.'

'I will indeed.' Anna's smile was loving. 'Though why you didn't tell me . . .'

'Tell you?' asked Franz, but a ferocious gesture from his wife sent him hurrying from the room.

'Quite right,' said Anna. 'Not just the moment.'

Franz's rapidly assembled search-party came back as dusk fell to report that they had followed Minette's carriage as far as Lake Constance and learned there that she had bribed the captain of one of the lake ferries to take her across that night.

'Oh, well, she's safe at least. That's something.' Joseph had returned late in the afternoon. 'I must say I rather hoped she would decide to leave before the winter, but one must regret the scrambling way she has done it. What, precisely, did she say to you, Martha?'

'She said she could take a hint when it was thrown in her face. But there was something else. Just as she was going. I asked if Napoleon might not be angry, and she said on the contrary he would be delighted to see her. And hear her news. As if – ' she hesitated.

'She had something useful to tell him,' Joseph finished the sentence for her. 'I do wonder what.'

'I doubt we'll know till spring,' said Franz cheerfully. 'The searchers said the pass was desperately difficult, coming back.'

'And it's snowing again,' said Max. 'Do I take it you gave Minette the hint to leave?' he asked Joseph. 'Because if so we all owe you our thanks.'

'Do you know,' said Martha, surprising herself as much as the rest of them. 'I believe I shall miss her?' And then wished she had not called attention to herself. Franz's report of the faint that had fatally delayed her intervening to stop Minette had got her a very close look from Joseph, but, to her relief, no comment.

'Then I am sorry I hunted her away,' said Joseph now. 'But, Martha, as your resident doctor, may I suggest that someone who fainted this morning should perhaps go early to bed tonight? Franz, take her away and see to it. And, Martha – ' With a very friendly look. 'I should have thought of this sooner; I'm ashamed. I'll come to you, in the morning, for the day's plans, not you to me. At ten, perhaps?'

'Thank you.' How long had he known? It was certainly more than time she told Franz.

Anna was waiting in their apartment, a loving scold at the ready, but Franz sent her away before she could get started. 'Now,' he had seated Martha in a chair, his arm around her shoulders. 'This faint of yours. Not just your line, surely.' He paused, looking down at her. 'Martha?'

'Yes?' She settled more comfortably against his arm.

'Am I being a hopeful fool?'

She turned to smile up at him. 'Well, if you are, Anna and I are too.'

'And Joseph? One tends to forget he's a doctor, now he's a prince. Well, we have our orders. I am to look after you and you are to take care of yourself.'

'An heir for Lissenberg?'

'No, my darling, our son.'

'Or – I hesitate to suggest it – our daughter?'

'Dearly welcome either way.' He pulled her close for a long, gentle kiss.

It snowed again next day and Prince Joseph dismissed his men early from the road works. Returning to the palace, he found Baron Hals watching for him. 'Lady Cristabel is here, highness. Asking to see you. Says it's urgent.'

'Lady Cristabel?' He looked down at himself. 'Urgent? She won't mind my wet clothes. I'll see her in the study. At once.' And when she appeared: 'What is it? What can I do for you?'

'It's Desmond.' She blushed crimson, then, as it faded, he saw how pale she was. 'He's vanished.'

'Vanished?'

'Nobody has seen him for two days. Since yesterday morning. I'd not have troubled you, highness, if I had not learned that Minette de Beauharnais left unexpectedly yesterday.'

'Don't call me highness!'

'It's your title. Don't make it harder for me. I saw him dancing with Minette the night before last.' She flashed him a straight, furious glance. 'Wooing her, the way I've seen him woo so many fools. Like myself.'

'Don't.' What could he say? 'But – you think he has gone with her? Why would she have taken him? Not, surely, on one night's wooing. Though it's true.' He was talking as much to himself as to her. 'I had made her very angry. I suggested she go,' he explained.

'Did you? Yes, that would have made her furious, poor Minette. And she danced the next dance with him.' Again the fiery blush as she realised she had revealed that she had been watching him and Minette.

166

'She said something to Martha.' His colour was high too. 'Something that sounded like a threat. Napoleon would welcome her, she said, and the news she brought. I've been worrying about that. But how could Fylde have known – ' He stopped short.

'About the road?' She took the wind quite out of his sails. 'That it goes in the wrong direction? You really did not know that secret was out? Has been for two days, since you started blasting? One of those Lissenberg secrets everyone knows and nobody mentions. I would have thought Desmond – and the French officers of course – was probably the only person who was unaware of what you were doing. But, if he found out somehow . . . He might well have thought it a valuable enough bit of information to pave his way with Napoleon. We had had an offer from Vienna,' she explained. 'His doing. I refused to go. He longed to. He was afraid of the winter here . . . He likes his comforts, Desmond. And, if Minette smiled at him . . . He thought himself irresistible to women . . . Why am I talking like this? As if he was gone? He might just have gone to Brundt, on one of his impulses. But we had an important rehearsal today. Franz was furious.'

'Franz should have told me.'

'Why? We thought it was just Desmond being Desmond. We didn't know then that no one had seen him. Don't you see? Maria thought he was with me. I was sure he was with Maria. He would not have spent the night in Brundt. So, where did he spend it?'

'Not with Minette. I sent after her to make sure she was safe. She crossed the border and went on board the ferry with only her men and her maid. She's gone, that's one thing certain, no stopping her now. And the very fact that she went so suddenly does make one think – '

'That she had learned something. To make up to Napoleon for her failure to marry you. I take it that is how you made her so angry? I'm only surprised she didn't decide to stay and have another try for poor Max. You're laughing?'

'I'm afraid I told her that was no use either.'

'Now I do wonder if you were right about that. You told her he was still wearing the willow for me? He's not, you know. He got over me a long time ago, just hasn't noticed it yet. A pity she's gone, really; I'd been beginning to wonder . . . But I'll tell you one thing, if she has taken Desmond with her – ' she ignored his protest, 'disguised as one of her men, maybe? He's an actor, remember; he could do it. But – if she has, she'll keep him in line. She's got a great deal of sense, Minette. If he has been indulging himself in the idea of becoming Napoleon's nephew-in-law he's in a fool's paradise. Minette is no green girl; she values herself highly, and why should she not?'

'She's younger than you, surely?'

'In years. But what I am trying to say is that I think your secret is probably safe with Desmond for the time being. He'll keep it to himself, as a bargaining point, until they catch up with Napoleon.'

'By which time the pass will be well and truly closed.' He looked out at steadily falling snow. 'I'd better question my men again. Would you mind staying? Something they said might identify Fylde to you.'

'Yes.' It was odd, she thought, how neither of them referred to Desmond as her husband. But then this entire conversation was strange beyond belief.

The two messengers were sure that Fylde had not been in Minette's little party. 'She came with a coachman, two men and a maid; she left with them; the papers were all in order. There was just one odd thing, it didn't seem worth mentioning before.' The two men had obviously been talking between themselves. 'The official who passed them through said something about a boy who should have been with her, and wasn't. And Mademoiselle de Beauharnais laughed about it and said the poor boy had got left behind. The party seemed to think this very funny, the man said.'

'A boy?' Joseph looked at Cristabel; they both thought about the stalwart tenor who would soon be portly, and Cristabel blushed furiously, then spoke. 'Not Desmond, that's for sure. But do you remember Minette's maid? Why should you? You probably never noticed her. A tiny little shrew of a French girl. She could pass as a boy easily enough, and have you ever heard Desmond sing falsetto?'

'He'd have been the maid?'

'I think so. I wonder . . . Poor Desmond. He's such a fool!

168

Do you think – would you mind? Could you send out a search-party?'

'You think Minette took drastic steps to keep him in line?'

'It could have happened.' she said soberly. 'And if so he has been out there in the snow for a day and a night.'

'And it's almost dark now. I'm afraid no search-party will be possible until the morning. I'm sorry! But they shall go out at first light, I promise.'

'Thank you. Poor Desmond,' she said again, and rose. 'I must go back to the hostel; maybe I'll find him there fresh from a long night at the gaming tables.'

'If you do, send at once.'

'Of course. I do thank you, prince.'

'You haven't asked me why I decided to change the route of the road,' Joseph said.

'No. I thought it none of my business.' And then, smiling for the first time. 'But I confess I long to know.'

'Thank you.' He was aware that they were talking in much more than words. 'It's the Lissenbergers,' he said now. 'This extraordinary cohesion among them. Well – imagine anywhere else, a secret known to everyone and mentioned by none. It makes sense about the Lissenbergers. I knew that the minute you told me. I've been learning it all summer, as I learned my way round the country. You called me spy and traitor once. Well, you were half right. I was a spy, but you can't be a traitor to a cause you don't know.'

'And now you do?'

'Well, I know Lissenberg a little now. And, if I can help it, I'm not going to let it be lost in Napoleon's military empire. That's what would happen, I'm sure, if the road went the way he intended. With Switzerland as a barrier it will be another story. Mind you, I've a case ready to make out to Napoleon, in the spring. If I'm lucky, and he hears it first from me, I might even convince him. It's an easier route, will cost less, take less time, be cheaper to maintain. I managed to convince his engineers, but then they are engineers, not military strategists. And they don't know much about our export trade.'

'It always comes back to that,' she said. 'Did you know that Napoleon himself saw to it that Lissenberg remained independent under the treaty of Rastatt?'

'Did he? Well, that's encouraging at least.' He held out a hand. 'Am I forgiven, Cristabel?'

'Forgiven?' She made herself ignore the hand. If she let him touch her, anything might happen. 'Long ago. What else could you do?'

'What else could we do? Are you going to call on Martha? She is missing Mademoiselle de Beauharnais, I think.'

'Good gracious. Then I'll certainly stop and see her.' She was grateful to him for getting them so easily past the moment of tension. She smiled. 'I think you may find your brother Max misses her too.'

'Now there's a thought for the spring! Cristabel – '

But she had swept him a deep curtsy and turned away.

16

The snow slackened in the night, giving way to a brilliant blue morning, and the search-parties were just starting out when a hooded figure came in sight, ploughing through drifted snow at the turn of the mountain road.

'Fylde, do you think?' Joseph, leading the party, turned back to Franz, who had agreed to stay home with Martha.

'I don't think so.' Franz shook his head. 'Not tall enough. Look – it's one of the Fathers.'

'So it is! With news, I hope.' He had recognised the man now as a probationer who had jibbed at taking the Trappists' final vow of silence. He moved forward to greet him as an old friend. 'Heinz! What brings you out through this new snow?'

'We need a doctor – ' He paused, remembering. 'Highness! We've got a very sick man up there. Brother Anselm found him when he was tending the cow last night. He'd got as far as the outer fence, fallen there, lain in the snow God knows how long. We got him in, warmed him as best we could, but his breath rattles in his chest . . . He's not come round at all . . . We need help, highness. The brothers sent me to you.'

'Do you know who it is?'

'Brother Martin thinks it's the tenor from the opera house. He heard him once last summer. We're afraid for his voice, highness, as well as his life.'

'I'll come.' Joseph turned to tell a servant to fetch his medical bag. 'Franz, send down to Cristabel will you? Tell her that her husband is found. Don't let her try to come to him. The path is going to be bad enough for me. If I can I'll have him brought down to the palace, but I doubt I'll be able to. Any further exposure might kill him.'

'He must have been out long enough already, if he was not found till nightfall.'

171

'I'm afraid so. Tell her not to be too hopeful.'

'Hopeful?' The brothers exchanged a long look.

Desmond Fylde was lying on the bed that had been Joseph's during the summer he had spent with the Fathers. They had heaped him with all the coverings they could find, and put hot bricks to his feet, but he was still shivering convulsively. His breath came harsh and painfully and he looked an old man, Joseph thought, the vital spirit drained out of him.

He muttered to himself as Joseph examined him and sent for more hot bricks, a charcoal stove close to the bed, anything to get rid of his deadly chill. 'No use.' The words became intelligible at last, but the sunken eyes looked unseeingly past Joseph. 'I'm finished, done for. Better like this. Let me go, there's a good fellow. To be an old man, an old fool, sitting by someone else's fire?' He spoke as if every word hurt him. 'She mocked me. Threw me out! Into the snow . . . Only being civil . . . Threw me out . . . So cold . . . Going to the Fathers . . . Thinking of a story . . . Snowing all the time.' He paused for a moment, breathing heavily. 'She led me on! Of course she did. An Irish prince . . . I told her . . . Invade Ireland . . . Her uncle . . . Bitch! . . . Long line of Irish princes . . .' His eyes focused at last on Joseph. 'It's the doctor prince! A prince at my bedside. At my deathside. No!' He pushed away the offered hot drink. 'One prince to another – let me go. Nothing left . . . Laughed at . . . mocked . . . into the snow . . . used up . . . useless . . . the Hound of Ulster!'

Joseph fought for him all that day and all night, but with less and less hope. With no fight from within, no will to live, what chance could there be? Minette had destroyed some vital cog in Fylde's machinery, broken him with one ruthless gesture. By next morning, he had stopped muttering and the slow, painful breath was only a whisper.

Not long now, Joseph thought as the light grew, and looked up to see Cristabel standing in the doorway, dressed in one of her men's costumes, under a heavy fur coat. 'Is he – ?'

'Dying.' Joseph made room for her by the bed and she took Fylde's hand.

'He's so cold! What happened?'

'He did go with Minette. From what he said, she had him

172

thrown out of the carriage . . . He lost his way in the snow. Cristabel, he doesn't want to live . . .'

'No.' She looked down thoughtfully at the still figure on the bed, rubbing the cold hand between both her own. 'He wouldn't, not like this.'

'Cristabel?' Fylde's tired eyes opened.

'Yes.' She bent closer.

'I'm sorry. Such a fool . . . But tell him, tell your doctor prince she doesn't know . . . I never told her . . . not about the road . . . princes don't . . . Kiss me, my queen?'

She bent to do so, felt the effort he made, and then –

'He's gone,' said Joseph quietly.

'Ah, poor Desmond.' One long look, then she bent to close the staring eyes with a hand that shook just a little. 'I loved him, you know. Once. I'm glad I was here. But it was you I came for. There's trouble at the palace.'

'Trouble?'

'The French. They've taken over the palace. Moved in last night. Disarmed our guards . . . You weren't there . . . Luckily I'd stayed with Martha – Why had nobody told me about her? Max and Franz are under arrest, I think, but nobody bothered about us, just put a guard on the door. So I came through the tunnel. Martha told me about it. I didn't like it much, but we must go back that way. Surprise them.'

'I'd forgotten about that tunnel.' He had belatedly taken in that she was not covered in snow, then, looking down at the body, 'I'll tell them to bury him here, shall I? Before the ground freezes too hard.'

'Yes, please. Poor Desmond,' she said again. 'I'm glad you were with him. Thank you, Joseph.' She touched Fylde's cold forehead. 'We must hurry! Martha's alone.'

He gave the orders quickly and five minutes later they were in the tunnel. So much to say, and none of it could be said. He was almost glad that the going was so difficult. 'You were a heroine to manage this alone,' he told her, sighing with relief as he opened the door at the far end.

'Oh, heroines!' They were climbing the rough inner stair in the palace now and she pushed cautiously at the secret door into the royal apartments.

'Thank God!' Martha rose to greet them, hugged Cristabel

and turned to Joseph. 'What are we going to do? They've got Franz!'

'Do you know where he is?' He put a soothing hand on hers.

'Anna's trying to find out. He's being held hostage to make you give yourself up. If you don't, it will be the dungeons . . .'

'I wonder where they think I am,' said Joseph.

'Nobody's told them anything. I do know that.'

'And nobody will,' said Cristabel. 'If I know the Lissenbergers. But I wish I understood . . .'

'There are so few of the French. And no leader among the officers.' Joseph had been thinking about it too. 'Something must have panicked them.'

'Someone.' Martha had had time to think about it. 'Your father, do you think?'

'I don't know, but I was mad to leave him at Gustavsberg. I'm sorry, Martha . . . But they won't hurt Franz, I'm sure. They are civilised people after all, the French.'

'No one is entirely civilised when he's afraid,' said Martha.

'You're right. So we must reassure them. There's a guard on the outside door here, I take it?'

'Yes, but they've been very civil about it, I must say. Anna comes to and fro . . . Everyone seems to know . . . About me . . .'

'Good. I told you they were civilised. Fathers themselves, some of them, missing their wives. I wonder . . . Cristabel?'

'Yes?'

'Would there be a French officer's uniform in the wardrobe at the opera house?'

'Bound to be.'

'And someone who speaks good French?'

She thought for a moment. 'I could find someone.'

'Good. Dress him in uniform. Tell him to cut up through the vineyards, come down to the palace by the mountain road, exhausted, with a tale of a foundered horse and lost despatches . . . and an urgent summons from the Emperor. Every man needed for the siege of Vienna. Who would dare disobey that?'

'It's certainly worth a try,' said Cristabel. 'But how am I

174

to get down to the opera house? I'm afraid the French know about that tunnel. Everyone does.'

'Yes, a pity. But I think we can manage. I am about to emerge, very much the prince. Take control, if I can. It's worth a try. Straight from your husband's deathbed.' To Cristabel. 'Give her a handkerchief, Martha. The desolate widow. I'm sorry!' He had seen Cristabel flinch. 'We need Anna, Martha.'

'She should be here any minute.' She cocked her head, listening, gestured them to silence. 'And here she is.' They could hear Anna speaking to the guard outside as he opened the door for her.

'Oh, thank God!' Anna saw Joseph, closed the door firmly behind her. 'You're safe, highness!'

'For the moment. What's happening in the palace, Anna? And where are my brothers?'

'Prince Franz is in the armoury, under guard. I'm sorry – ' to Martha, 'they wouldn't let me see him. He's being held hostage for you, sir. They won't hurt him.' This to Martha again.

'And Max?'

'They've not got him. No one knows where he is. They are still looking.'

'He's the one who knows the palace best,' said Joseph. 'With a bit of luck he got clean away in the confusion when the French took over the castle. And that reminds me, the French officers, Anna. What are they doing?'

'Sir, I don't think they know what to do. They're all in the great hall . . . arguing. They're frightened, I think. I don't understand much French, more's the pity.'

'Time I went to them. They need a leader, and that's what I'm going to be. Can you get the guard away from the door, Anna? Just long enough for Lady Cristabel and me to get out without being seen?'

'Oh, I think so, sir,' said Anna cheerfully. 'He's not a bad chap, that guard. He's even learned a little Liss. If I can get him down to the end of the hall, could you slip out, quickly, while he's busy.'

'Admirable!' Nobody asked what the sentry would be busy doing. Joseph bent to kiss Martha on both cheeks. 'Take care

175

of yourself and our little Lissenberger, Martha. And I'll send Franz to you just as soon as I can.'

'Dear Joseph.' She smiled up at him mistily. 'I know you will.' She and Cristabel exchanged a quick hug. 'I've never said how sorry I am.'

'No time,' said Cristabel. 'Poor Desmond.'

The two of them slipped quickly down the corridor with just one amused glance for the sentry, who, with Anna in his arms, was totally oblivious. 'This way.' Joseph had studied his palace since taking it over and led the way quickly down a series of side passages, to emerge, suddenly, close to the dais in the great hall.

It was babel. So far as he could see, all the French officers were present, all frantically talking on a rising tide of noise. He took the steps of the dais in a stride. 'Silence!' The command, shouted in French, was almost instantly effective. 'What madness is this?' He went on over the last few fragments of anxious talk. 'What folly have you idiots been committing while I've been away at Monsieur Fylde's deathbed? Who is in charge at Lissenberg? Who at Brundt? Worst of all, who is watching Prince Gustav?' He singled out three faces in the crowd, beckoned them to him. 'You, you and you. What explanation can you give for leaving your posts?'

'It's a conspiracy, sir, a dangerous one.' The officer who had been in charge at Lissenberg hurried to explain himself. 'We were all to have been murdered in our beds. Last night, it was to have been. My friend here got the word – '

'Yes.' The man from Brundt took up the tale. 'By sheer good fortune one of my men overheard two of the conspirators. Bloodcurdling it was, he said. Everyone of us to be killed; no quarter; dead men tell no tales. Then you and Mademoiselle de Beauharnais were to be held hostage for Napoleon's pardon. There was no time to be lost, sir, you must see that. Last night, it was to have been. This was the only place we had a chance of holding out!'

'And who were these two dangerous conspirators?' asked Joseph. And then, 'But I am forgetting. Hals!' He had seen the baron, looking miserable, at the back of the crowd. 'Arrange a carriage for Lady Cristabel at once. Her husband has

176

just died; she needs to be at home.' Taking obedience for granted, he turned back to the French officer. 'The conspirators' names?'

'Two prominent citizens of Brundt, sir. Frau Schmidt, who is some kind of connection of your brother's, I believe. We've got Prince Franz safe under guard, in case he's involved. And a Jew, Ishmael Brodski.'

'I see.' He thought he was beginning to see a great deal. 'And who is guarding Prince Gustav?' He turned to the officer who had been in charge at Gustavsberg.

'My orders were just to come away, sir.' The man shuffled his feet.

Here was a complication Joseph had not thought of. What would Gustav do when he found himself free? But the conspirators at Brundt must have thought of this hazard; he must assume that they would have arranged for a Lissenberg guard to take over if the French should panic as they hoped. And as, amazingly, they had. At one overheard conversation between an old lady and a foreigner. But then the French must be accustomed to treachery and violence. And, he smiled to himself, Frau Schmidt and Ishmael Brodski were a formidable pair. He must play the hand they had dealt him for all it was worth. And, most important of all, he must keep the French officers occupied and give Cristabel time to find her messenger.

'Orders given by you?' He barked the question at the man from Brundt, the senior of the three officers.

'There was not a moment to be lost. We've got the palace well guarded, sir, but I reckon they won't try anything now they've lost the element of surprise.'

'It was to be last night you say?'

'Yes, at midnight. Throats cut in our beds! They could have done it too, sir, you must know that as well as I do. Total surprise! Who'd have thought it of these mild Lissenbergers? Pulled the wool over our eyes good and proper they have. Why, I myself – ' He paused, reddening, and Joseph remembered something he had heard about him and Maria, the seconda donna at the opera house. 'It don't bear thinking of,' he went on. 'And what we don't know, sir, if you'll forgive my saying so, is whether your brothers are involved or not. We've got

177

Franz, the one that was prince, safe in the guard-room here, but we can't find a trace of young Max. Which makes me a mite anxious, sir.' In the relief of sharing the problem with which he felt himself burdened he had forgotten any initial suspicions he might have had of Joseph. But then, why should he suspect him? Joseph had always been Napoleon's man, after all.

'He's probably hard at work down at the opera house, knows nothing about any of this. But fetch Prince Franz; it's time I talked to him.' It had to be done, but it was unbelievably dangerous. How much did Franz understand of what was happening, and, most important of all, in this crisis, would he trust him? Would he believe him to be acting for Lissenberg and not for Napoleon?

Franz looked exhausted, anxious and angry. All very dangerous emotions at this dangerous moment. If only I spoke Liss, thought Joseph, and then, no, that would be too risky, it must be French, to be understood by all. He looked his younger brother up and down as he stood between two French dragoons, hands tied behind his back. 'I have to ask you, Franz, if you are involved in this diabolical conspiracy of the Lissenbergers.'

'What diabolical conspiracy? Nobody has told me anything! They just burst in and tied me up. And what I want to know, Joseph, is how Martha is.'

Joseph very nearly told him, remembered at the last moment that so far as the French were concerned he did not know himself. 'Where is the princess?' he asked the officer from Brundt.

'In her own apartments, sir. Her maid's with her. We don't make war on ladies.'

'Even if they make war on you?' He turned to Franz. 'I'm sorry to tell you, Franz, that your foster mother seems to be involved in a fiendish plot against the French. She and Brodski were overheard planning it. The French were all to have been murdered in their beds last night. They took over the palace in self defence. Otherwise, none of them would have been alive this morning.' He said this very straight to Franz, who was watching him as if his life depended on it. Which it very likely did. All their lives.

178

'I can't believe it,' said Franz slowly at last. 'But – you, Joseph, what did they plan for you?'

'Minette and I were to be held hostages for Napoleon's pardon. That reminds me – ' He turned to the French officer. 'One thing you don't know – They'd have failed there. Mademoiselle de Beauharnais left two days ago. An urgent summons from her uncle, I understand. I would have been their only hostage, and not a very valuable one, I am afraid. I'm only valuable to Napoleon as a Lissenberger,' he reminded the French officers. 'But I wish I knew why the Emperor summoned his niece away so suddenly.' Here was an unexpectedly strong card in his hand and he played it for all he was worth. 'We all thought she would stay through the winter.'

'She's gone?' Amazed. 'But she was at the party . . .' They had all been at the party. It seemed a thousand years ago.

'She left the next day. I didn't see her, but I do know she went in a hurry. We were a little anxious for her, in fact. The road will be closed any moment now, I think, and then, here we are . . .' He paused a moment to let the unpalatable truth strike home, then went on, 'So we had best take counsel together as to how we are to hold Lissenberg, with our limited numbers, in the face of this shocking threat. Oh – and untie my brother's hands, for goodness sake. Anyone can see he is as amazed as the rest of us. Do you happen to know where Max is, Franz? Our friends have not managed to find him. I said I thought he was probably down at the opera house.'

'Very likely.' Franz shrugged. 'He usually is.' He was massaging his freed wrists. 'Have I your permission to go and see Martha, Joseph? I don't like to think of her alone at this anxious time.'

'Of course. But, please, a quick visit, just to reassure her. Then, there is something I want you to do for me, Franz. In their moment of crisis, these gentlemen appear to have left Gustavsberg unguarded. Take a small band of Lissenbergers. The palace guard – They're sound to a man – you need not have disarmed them – ' To the three French officers. 'And make sure that no harm has come to Prince Gustav.'

'Gladly.' The brothers exchanged a long, thoughtful look.

'And give my best regards to Princess Martha. Tell her she has nothing to fear, and urge her to take care of herself,

179

and of Lissenberg's future.' He turned back to the French officers. 'Now, gentlemen, let us consider what is best to do for Lissenberg's safety – and yours.'

But they had not got far with the insoluble problem of holding down a mountainous country apparently hell-bent on the most desperate kind of guerrilla warfare when there was a commotion outside and Baron Hals appeared. 'There's a man come down from the mountains, highness.' He ignored the French officers, addressing Joseph. 'From the Trappists. He says it's urgent. Will you see him?'

'At once.'

17

It was starting to snow again as Franz set out for Gustavsberg with a picked band from the palace guard. They were still in a state of shock and shame at having been taken so completely by surprise the night before. 'It all happened so fast,' was all they could say. 'And they were desperate, those Frenchmen.'

'They were frightened men. Thought they were all going to be murdered in their beds.'

'Pity we didn't think of it, really,' said one of the men. 'I'd be happy to see the back of them, I don't know about you, sir?'

'Well, of course,' said Franz.

'And your brother? Prince Joseph? That's what we need to know. I reckon if we'd been sure about him we'd have put up a fight last night. But there he is thick as thieves with them this morning.' It was not exactly a question, but intended as one.

'Of course he is!' Franz had not wasted his time with Martha. 'He's taken command in the hopes of persuading them to leave peacefully before the road is closed.'

'He'll never manage that surely, sir?'

'He managed to take over Lissenberg,' said Franz.

'And you trust him?'

'Absolutely. As he trusts me. And now we had better save our breath for the road.' They had reached the point where the Gustavsberg road branched off, and no clearing had been done. From then on it was a hard, breathless struggle through newly drifted snow and there was no more talk.

They had crossed the open ridge and started down the thickly forested slope towards Gustav's castle when Franz stopped, raised a hand for silence. At first, all they could hear was silence itself, the deep quiet of soft-falling snow, then, from below, somewhere in the thick of the forest, came the sound of a voice, carrying strangely through the great quietness. They were silent for a minute, then heard it again. 'Coming this way,' breathed one of the men.

'Yes.' Franz kept his own voice to a whisper. 'No way to tell how many. Into the trees. Don't move, don't fire, nothing till I give the sign. Pass the word along. And, quietly!' They had the advantage of the ground, the snow-covered track sloped away from them, visible for a hundred yards or more.

Impossible to tell how far away the other party was, nor how many they were. It was cold, standing in the steadily falling snow, but Franz was pleased with the stoic silence of his little band. Not a word, not a movement betrayed their presence to the men they could now hear approaching up the track. Not many of them, Franz thought now, and not coming at all in stealth. But then, who would expect to meet anyone on this seldom used track?

He cursed the veil of snow as the little group of figures emerged, dimly seen through it, at the turn of the road. Six or seven of them, coming steadily on, not talking much, with the snow blowing in their faces. Talking Liss? He thought so. They were within easy hearing distance now. He whispered a command, stepped out into the path, raised a hand and spoke in Liss: 'Stop, or we fire. We outnumber you more than two to one.' His men were forming up silently behind him, visible proof of his point.

'How very warlike!' The other voice was pitched to carry against the snow. 'We've no intention of fighting you, Franz!'

'Max! How in the world?' The two parties met, coalesced, and the twins clasped mittened hands, briefly, warmly. 'You've come from Gustavsberg?'

'With grim news, I'm afraid. Our father's dead.'

'Gustav? Dead?'

'Murdered. When the French withdrew yesterday he summoned his servants, ordered them to march on the opera house. He meant, I think, in the confusion, to take it over – you and me with it, and Cristabel – hold us to ransom.'

'For Lissenberg?'

'I suppose so. He must have been more than a little mad, to think he had the slightest chance.'

'But what happened?'

'They turned on him, his own servants, in his own hall . . . A

182

horrible end.' He was silent for a moment, both of them thinking of the father who had brought this on himself. 'I got there too late to save him, but in time, thank God, to protect the Countess and her children. Princess, I should say, poor lady.'

'But how come you were there at all?' Franz shifted cold feet in the snow.

'By good luck. I was in Joseph's study when the French arrived last night. Heard what was happening; knew there was no way I could stop them. I've lived in that palace most of my life, got myself out by ways of my own and rounded up a few old friends. I was a little anxious about what our father might do after the French left.'

'As well you might be. But what have you done with the murderers?'

'Left them at Gustavsberg under guard. We hadn't enough men to make it safe to try and bring them to the castle. Besides, what is going on there? Does Joseph need help?'

'I hope not, but if things are under control at Gustavsberg, we should be getting back. I'll tell you as we go. I'm glad to see you are just as sure of Joseph as I am.' He was aware of the men around them, listening.

'Oh yes. I think I always have been, since he found out who he was. There was only one way for him to go then, being Joseph. And then, when word got out about the road, I knew I had been right. Satisfactory, it was.'

'Yes.' They were trudging side-by-side up hill through the snow. 'That's when I was sure, but Martha always was, right from the start.'

'Not Cristabel,' said Max. 'I've sometimes thought she hated him.'

'Have you? I wonder . . .' Franz was silent for a moment, then: 'Her husband is dead, Max.'

'What?'

'Last night.' He described what had happened, briefly.

'Oh, the poor, hopeless fellow,' said Max, and they were both quiet for a while.

'You again!' Joseph looked with genuine surprise at Brother Heinz as he was brought through the crowded hall to the dais. 'What now?'

'Highness, I am sent to report another casualty of this storm. The Fathers thought you should know at once, and the French gentlemen too, since it concerns them.'

'Do you speak French?'

'I'm afraid not, highness. Only German and Liss. I'm just a simple Lissenberger.'

If there was such an animal, Joseph thought. 'Then speak German and I will translate for you.' He turned to the French officers. 'This man has come down from the monastery. He says he has news that concerns you. Of another victim of the weather. Shall I translate for you?' And, taking agreement for granted. 'Go on, Heinz.'

'He came at first light this morning. He'd been out all night . . . His horse foundered, somewhere on the slope up from Lake Constance . . . Fell with him suddenly. Hurt his chest . . . The strap of his wallet broke, he says, it fell away into the snow, down the slope, won't be seen till spring. He's an imperial messenger,' Heinz explained, and waited for Joseph to translate.

'And the message?' Joseph asked, having done so. 'Does he know what it is?'

'Oh, yes. The Emperor is outside Vienna, needs more men. You are to send him every man you can spare. The Russians have joined forces with the Austrians against him.' Joseph, translating swiftly for the French officers, thought the speech very obviously learned by heart, but then, so it would have been, even had the message been genuine. He turned back to Heinz. 'The messenger,' he asked. 'How is he? If I come, could I help him? Could I question him?'

'The brothers say no, highness. No hope. He told us all this when he first came, they got some brandy down him, it helped for a while, he got his message out, then, suddenly, something happened . . . He's not been conscious since . . . It's only a matter of time, we think. And, highness, it's snowing again. I was told to come back as soon as you can spare me, for fear of not being able to get through.'

He had been well coached, Joseph thought. Once again, he felt Cristabel's hand held out to help him. And, he was sure, if he should fight his way through the snow, with one of the French officers for witness, there would be a convincingly helpless 'dying' man to interview. Fruitlessly, of course. Once again, he translated for the Frenchmen, then addressed the three senior officers. 'I think we have no choice in the matter,' he told them. 'The Emperor needs you; I must let you go. It's too late tonight, I am afraid, but you must make ready to start at first light in the morning. Every hour will make the pass more dangerous. Frankly, I had been wondering whether I should not send you out anyway, for all our sakes. This order comes as a relief to me. I think I may deal better with the Lissenbergers on my own.'

'You won't come with us?'

'No. It's my duty to stay here, hold Lissenberg.' He did not say for whom. 'You will report the situation fully to the Emperor, and I will write to him, of course.' Though what he would say was very much another question. It was going to be a busy night.

'But the engineers,' said the officer from Brundt. 'What of them?'

It was a question Joseph had very much hoped no one would remember to ask. In their precipitate retreat, the French had forgotten all about the engineers, hard at work in the cutting on the other side of Brundt, and it had been an immense relief to Joseph since these were the one group of Frenchmen who knew exactly which way the road was going. But they were enthusiasts more for their work than for their Emperor, and had so far been too busy to bother about the implications of the line the road was taking. 'Oh, they must stay,' he said now. 'I'll see they are protected. I promised the Emperor the road would be through next year. They must be here to start work first thing in the spring. No need to fear for them, gentlemen. All Lissenberg has a stake in that road.' And that, at least, was true.

He was struggling with the seventh draft of an impossible letter to Napoleon when Baron Hals appeared. 'Prince Franz has returned, highness. He asks to see you. At once.'

'He's alone?' Here was something strange. 'Send him in.'

'I left the others at the hostel.' Franz had told his tale in the fewest possible words. 'I thought it safest.'

'And came to share my fate. Thank you, Franz.'

'Martha is here.'

'She knows you're safe?'

'I sent a message. But the French? Are they really going?'

'Unless anything goes wrong overnight. Hold your breath, Franz, and pray. Anything could burst this bubble! You were absolutely right not to bring anyone else here. Just one casual word could make them realise how they are being hoodwinked.'

'Then we had better not speak until they are gone!'

'No. Franz, where is Cristabel?'

'Still up with the Trappists. Just in case the French decide to go and interview the "messenger". Rather a young one, but I'd trust her to put on a deathbed scene that would convince anyone. By sheer good luck, Brother Heinz was down at the opera house. She sent him up through the vineyards with the message, went up through the tunnels herself, in case the French should insist on seeing Napoleon's man.'

'Thank God for Cristabel,' said Joseph. 'Franz, help me with this letter to Napoleon! It's a devil! Must give nothing away, in case they open it . . .'

'Not easy,' said Franz. 'I suppose it depends a little on what you want to tell him.'

'But that's not the question. You must see that. The question, surely, is what Lissenberg wants to tell him.'

'I don't see why you shouldn't know that as well as anyone else. Better.'

'Then I shall tell him Lissenberg means to be a friendly neutral. Will that make Cristabel very angry, do you think?'

'Cristabel?'

'As an Englishwoman.' Could Joseph possibly be blushing?

'Oh, I see. No, I think Cristabel thinks, now, as an artist, not a patriot. Of any kind.'

'Pity we haven't got more like her,' said Joseph.

There was a savage frost that night, but no snow fell, and the French marched out in good order next morning, played off with a spirited rendering of the 'Marseillaise' by the palace musicians. They had the best guides in Lissenberg to see them safe over the pass and down to Lake Constance. After they had left, no one said much. They might still find the pass impossible and come back.

'But I doubt it.' Paying Martha his daily visit as if nothing had happened, Joseph had found Franz with her. 'They were badly frightened men. I think they will prefer a snowdrift or two to being murdered in their beds.'

'What savages they must think us,' said Martha.

'We Lissenbergers?' Franz's voice was very loving. 'But, I think, my darling, they are judging by themselves. How many of them, I wonder, lost a loved one or a friend during their Reign of Terror, ten years ago. It's not a long time to forget anything so savage. You Americans managed things better with your revolution.'

'I'm not an American any more,' Martha smiled at them both. 'I find I am a Lissenberger.'

'And Cristabel?' asked Joseph.

'You'd better ask her,' said Martha. 'But not today. She said she would stay at the monastery until tomorrow, just in case the French took it into their heads to pay a call on their dying messenger.' She looked out of the window. 'I ought to go and see Lady Helen, she will be anxious.'

'Send for her,' said Joseph. 'You are supposed to be looking after yourself. Or rather, I will send, for her and for Max. We three have a lot to think about, Franz.'

'What I want to know,' said Franz, 'is just what the Lissenbergers are thinking. What they expected would happen after they put that fright into the French. After all, Joseph, for all they knew, you might have scuttled off over the mountains too!'

'Those poor French,' said Martha. 'What will the Emperor do to them, do you think?'

'I wrote him a very politic letter,' Joseph told her. 'Saying a great deal, and nothing at all. With a bit of luck, he'll need the men – he always does – and by spring this storm in a mountain valley will be forgotten. Or remembered as unimportant.'

'Just the same,' said Franz. 'I'll be glad when the guides get back with the news that the French are across the lake. What will you do if they come back, Joseph? I rather expected to see the guard out in full strength, just in case.'

'Good gracious, no,' said Joseph. 'That would be to admit I had deceived them. No, I thought I'd ask them, very civilly, if they would be so good as to hold Gustavsberg for me for the winter.'

'Clever,' said Franz. 'I knew you'd think of something.'

But the long day dragged on with no sign of the French, and at last, just towards dusk, the guides returned to report that they had seen them safe down the last slope to Lake Constance.

'No chance of their starting to cross until morning,' said Franz, 'and it will take several days, I'm afraid, for their numbers to get over. Suppose they should meet a real imperial messenger, with real news?'

'It's snowing again,' said Joseph. 'The guides say the pass will be closed by morning.'

'We're shut up here for the winter!' Lady Helen had arrived expecting to find Cristabel at the palace and had spent the day grumbling to Martha about her mysterious absence. 'I had so hoped I might be able to get my poor Cristabel down to Venice – to her mother for the rest and care she needs.'

'Rest and care? Lady Cristabel?' asked Joseph. 'You think that is what she needs?'

'Of course. How should a man understand? After the summer she has had – the way that man treated her – you cannot surely imagine that she will be able to go on singing in your opera house as if nothing had happened? Associating with the seconda donna? Do you know where that man spent his last night in Lissenberg?'

'No,' said Joseph. 'Nor do I wish to. And it is no kindness on your part, Lady Helen, to keep reminding your niece of the past. That's the way to turn her into a moping widow. Not her line at all. What she needs, just now, is to be occupied, to be needed. As indeed she is. This is not going to be an easy winter, here in Lissenberg.'

'I should rather think not,' said Lady Helen. 'They'll be murdering all foreigners in their beds next, not just the French. That's what I told Cristabel. If she's got any sense, maybe she's safe away after all. The monastery is almost at the top of the pass. What's to stop her getting out, while she's up there, and the going is still good?'

'She'd never leave you, Lady Helen,' said Martha.

'I left her,' said Lady Helen. 'What is there to keep her here, now? I'll not blame her if she's gone to her mother, left me here to face the winter alone.'

'Not alone, Lady Helen,' said Martha. 'I need you.' She had seen Joseph's face go grey at Lady Helen's suggestion. How could she have been so blind? All kind of things made sudden sense. 'But she won't have gone,' she said with absolute certainty. 'She knows we all need her. Yes, Baron Hals?'

'There's a deputation, highness.' He looked at all three princes, spoke to Joseph. 'From Lissenberg. They came up through the tunnel, ask you to see them. They are in the great hall.'

'How many?' asked Joseph. 'And who?'

'Just six of them. Three from Lissenberg, three from Brundt. Frau Schmidt – ' He named the others.

'Good.' Joseph exchanged a satisfied glance with Franz. 'We'll see them, Hals, but not in the great hall. Take them to my office, arrange for refreshments, we will be with them directly. All of us, I think. Martha, are you well enough?'

'Of course I am. There's nothing wrong with me. And Lady Helen will keep me company . . .'

'I'll keep you company, Martha.' Cristabel had emerged from the secret door while their attention was centred on Hals. 'And thanks for your confidence.' She turned to Lady Helen. 'You can't really have thought I would leave you, aunt?'

'How was I to know what to think!' And then, scandalised. 'You cannot be proposing to meet the delegation dressed like that?'

'I'm not meeting the delegation.' Cristabel glanced down at her doublet and hose, now the worse for a good deal of wear. 'That's the princes' business. But if I can appear like this at the opera house, I don't see why I can't at the palace.'

'Of course.' Joseph dismissed it. 'But there is something I must say to you first.' He turned to Martha. 'May I beg the use of your room for a few minutes? And, Franz, tell Hals we'll be with the delegation immediately, will you?'

'You wish to see Lady Cristabel alone?' Lady Helen sounded

both amazed and outraged as Martha rose to her feet and made to usher her out.

'Yes, alone. If she does not object?'

'Why should I?' Cristabel made him a little stage bow. 'My employer, after all, Aunt Helen. And we should not be keeping the Lissenbergers waiting.'

'Thank you,' Joseph said to her as the door closed gently behind Max.

'No need for thanks.' She took a step forward into the room. 'I am absolutely devoured with curiosity, prince. What question is important enough to keep the Lissenbergers waiting?'

'If you don't know, it's not worth the asking. But you do know. We've no time for pretence, Cristabel. No need for it, either. You must have known how totally I have been yours, ever since that first day, that first touch of your hand. Crazy, perhaps, but there it is. And now, in a minute, I am to meet the Lissenbergers and make a decision that will affect my whole life. How can I do it, without consulting you first?'

'You mean, you would say no?'

'If that was what you wanted. Yes I would. Do you think me madly over confident that I assume they are going to offer me Lissenberg?'

'Oh, no,' she said. 'Not now they understand you. Now you understand yourself.'

'You were terribly angry with me.'

'Yes. I thought you had betrayed yourself, as well as the rest of us. I'm glad I was wrong. But, Joseph,' when had she used his name before? 'You are forgetting something. I am no princess for Lissenberg. A widow! Of two days. And such a widow. Of such a husband. Publicly, here in Lissenberg. You'd be a laughing stock.'

'If they think that, I'm no prince for them. If they do offer it to me, I shall stipulate absolute freedom to marry as I please. No more than that, and no less. And let them think what they will.'

'And if they say no?'

He smiled, and took her hand. 'I am afraid I may be reduced to living on the earnings of my brilliant wife! But they'll offer it to me, you'll see. Cristabel, you've helped me so. You're not going to fail me now!'

190

'You won't mind my singing?' Their hands had touched, clapsed, now he was pulling her towards him.

'You are your singing.' He bent to kiss her and time stood still.

'Just the same.' She freed herself, gently, at last. 'We should see these Lissenbergers.'

'Bless you for that we! Cristabel, how soon?'

'Ah, my dear,' she smiled up at him. 'We'll have to consult Aunt Helen about that.'